"Jessica, what's wrong?" Sam asked, catching up to her in the parking lot and putting a hand on her shoulder.

"What are you doing here?" Jessica demanded, turning to face him. "I thought you had to study tonight!"

"I did have to study. But I finished early and decided I'd drive down to the Dairi Burger to see you. You *did* tell me you'd be here, didn't you?"

"Well, yes. But I didn't expect to get here and find you flirting with Paula behind my back!"

"Flirting? Is that what you think? We were only talking, Jessica."

Jessica hugged herself and stared into the darkness at the other end of the parking lot. "You never look at me that way when we're *only talking.*"

"Jessica, I don't know what's wrong with you lately. You seem to go off the deep end whenever Paula's involved. It's not like you to be so paranoid."

"Sam," said Jessica, trying to stay calm, "I am *not* paranoid. Paula is trying to sabotage me somehow. You've got to believe me!"

"Jessica, you're making me angry. I see what's going on. Your little protégé is ready to make her own friends, and you can't handle that."

Sam stalked away, but halfway across the parking lot he turned around and yelled back at her, "What do you want, Jess? To control Paula? She's not your puppet, you know!"

"No," whispered Jessica. "But I may be hers."

The SWEET VALLEY HIGH series, published by Bantam Books. Ask your bookseller for any titles you have missed.

SHE'S NOT WHAT SHE SEEMS

Written by
Kate William

Created by
FRANCINE PASCAL

BANTAM BOOKS
NEW YORK • TORONTO • LONDON • SYDNEY • AUCKLAND

SHE'S NOT WHAT SHE SEEMS
A BANTAM BOOK 0 553 29849 6

Originally published in U.S.A. by Bantam Books

First publication in Great Britain

PRINTING HISTORY
Bantam edition published 1993

Sweet Valley High is a registered trademark of Francine Pascal.

Conceived by Francine Pascal

Produced by Daniel Weiss Associates, Inc., 33 West 17th Street, New York, NY 10011

Cover art by James Mathewuse

Bantam Books are published by Transworld Publishers Ltd., 61–63 Uxbridge Road, Ealing, London W5 5SA, in Australia by Transworld Publishers (Australia) Pty. Ltd., 15–25 Helles Avenue, Moorebank, NSW 2170, and in New Zealand by Transworld Publishers (N.Z.) Ltd., 3 William Pickering Drive, Albany, Auckland.

Printed and bound in Great Britain by Cox & Wyman Ltd., Reading, Berks.

One

"Look like the innocent flower, but be the serpent under it!" Jessica Wakefield's voice rose dramatically from behind her bedroom door.

Her twin sister, Elizabeth, was standing in the bathroom that separated their rooms. Elizabeth stopped for a moment to listen. Then she pushed open the door. "I'm trying to study," she said. "Would you please keep it down in there?"

Jessica whirled around to face her. "You could knock, you know."

"I did knock—three times," said Elizabeth. "You were too busy plotting the king's murder to pay attention."

"Well, it's a very important murder," said Jessica. "It's going to make me a star!"

"Perhaps you could twinkle a little more quietly." Elizabeth said, a smile spreading across

1

her face. She never could stay mad at Jessica for long.

"I'm rehearsing *Macbeth*, and you want me to be quiet! I thought English was your favorite subject."

"It is," Elizabeth answered. "But right now I'm trying to study French verbs, not English literature." Elizabeth turned to leave. As she did a pair of jeans became entwined around her ankle. As usual, most of her twin's large and trendy wardrobe was lying wrinkled on the floor.

"How do you live in this mess?" Elizabeth asked, kicking her foot free.

"What mess?" asked Jessica, her blue-green eyes wide.

Elizabeth shook her head. Only Jessica could stand in the middle of such a disaster area and ask, "What mess?"

The sixteen-year-old twins were identical in appearance, with turquoise eyes, a tiny dimple in their left cheek, and perfect southern California tans. They both had long, sun-streaked blond hair, but Elizabeth usually pulled hers back in a casual style, while Jessica preferred loose, sexy waves.

Both twins wore a size six, but Elizabeth's taste in clothes was far more conservative than her sister's. Jessica, who loved being the center of attention, usually wore the newest, flashiest fashions. But she certainly wasn't dressed that way now, Elizabeth noted. Jessica wore a long, demure nightgown, and had her hair pinned up on top of her head.

"Wait a minute," said Elizabeth. "That's *my*

new nightgown you're wearing—the one you said you'd never be caught dead in!"

"I know," said Jessica. "It *is* hideous. But you don't mind if I borrow it to practice being Lady Macbeth, do you? I need to get in the mood," she explained. "It's the longest, flowingest thing I could find—even if it does have zero sex appeal."

"OK, OK," Elizabeth gave in. "On one condition: Promise to keep your voice down. I need to concentrate on my irregular verbs."

"I don't know what the big deal is," said Jessica. "You don't need to study; you always get straight A's. And I have to be loud. A great actress has to project her voice so it can be heard to the back of the theatre."

"Project it somewhere else!" said Elizabeth. "How about the garage? Besides, shouldn't you be studying for the French test, too?"

"Are you crazy? This is only Sunday night," said Jessica. "The test isn't until Wednesday morning. I don't have to study until—'tomorrow, and tomorrow, and tomorrow.' Or maybe I should say, 'Tuesday night, and Tuesday night, and Tuesday night'!"

Elizabeth tried to look stern. "I know the teachers said they'd be lenient about schoolwork with cast members," she said. "But you aren't a cast member yet. Auditions don't even start until Tuesday. You shouldn't let your schoolwork slide completely."

"Stop playing big sister with me," said Jessica. "Remember, you're four *minutes* older, not four years!"

Elizabeth smiled wryly. She often did feel like the much older sister—the sensible twin. Jessica was the one who always chose having fun over being responsible.

Despite their differences, both twins were among the most popular students in the junior class at Sweet Valley High. But they were popular among different groups. Elizabeth thought Jessica's friends, especially Lila Fowler and Amy Sutton, were silly and superficial. Elizabeth preferred her own best friend, Enid Rollins. Jessica thought that Enid was hopelessly dull. In fact, she thought that most of Elizabeth's friends were entirely too serious.

Jessica was seldom serious about anything. She always said she didn't like being tied down by one activity. She thought Elizabeth was crazy to spend so much time writing for Sweet Valley High's student newspaper, *The Oracle*.

Until recently, Jessica had even criticized her sister for her devotion to her steady boyfriend, Todd Wilkins. Jessica had never believed in being serious about one boy—until she had started dating Sam Woodruff, a senior at nearby Bridgewater High.

But Elizabeth had to admit that Jessica did seem serious about this play. Jessica had been in school plays before, and both girls had recently acted in a television soap opera. But this was different. Jessica was absolutely determined to play Lady Macbeth. And Elizabeth knew her sister well enough to know that when Jessica made up

4

her mind to do something, there was no standing in her way.

Unfortunately, Jessica also seemed determined to keep her sister from having any peace tonight.

"Help me, Liz. You're good at this stuff. The language doesn't make any sense. Like here—what does it mean when I say, 'Only look up clear. To alter favor ever is to fear'?" She held out the book.

"To look up clear means to look innocent. Lady Macbeth is telling her husband that if he has a guilty expression on his face, people will suspect something," Elizabeth explained. "But Jessica, I've heard you practicing, and you sound great. You don't need any help. You'll do fine in the audition."

"No I won't. I really, really need you, Liz. I'll just die if I don't get this part. But I won't be able to impress a famous theatre director like David Goodman if I don't understand what I'm saying. Would you help me with some other lines tonight—please?"

"Jessica, I told you, I need to study. I'm sorry, but schoolwork is more important."

"More important?" cried Jessica. "*Nothing* is more important than this play. Where have you been, Mars? The posters have been plastered all over school for more than a week. And you were at the assembly Friday where Mr. Goodman explained the whole thing."

"I know, I know," said Elizabeth. "He's picked Sweet Valley High this year for his annual student theatre production. He's casting the major roles this week, in three rounds of auditions. Then he'll hold tryouts next week for the minor parts. So?"

"The kids who are in this production will be seen by theatre critics—and maybe even talent scouts!" Jessica said. "Liz, this is my big chance to be discovered as an actress. You've got to help me!"

"All right," said Elizabeth with a sigh. "I give up. You've got me for *one hour*." She shoved aside a damp towel and sat on Jessica's unmade bed. "But then I'm going back to my French book, and you have to promise to rehearse more quietly." She took the script from Jessica. "Where do you want to start?"

"Will the famous actress lower herself to talk to us?" Amy Sutton asked Lila Fowler as they stood near their lockers the next morning. She gestured toward Jessica, who was slowly walking down the hall toward them. Jessica carried an open book and moved her lips silently as she read.

"Is Jessica Wakefield *reading a book*?" asked Lila in a loud voice. "Somebody take her temperature!"

"You know, it *could* be Jessica," replied Amy. "But I'm not sure if I would recognize her. It seems like *ages* since I've seen her."

Jessica looked up suddenly. "Oh, hi!" she said. "I didn't notice you two."

"Well, that's only fair," said Lila, "seeing

as how *we* didn't notice *you* yesterday at the mall."

"The mall?" asked Jessica.

"Remember the Valley Mall?" asked Lila. "Your home away from home? The place where you were supposed to meet Amy and me at one o'clock yesterday afternoon?"

"Sorry. I didn't have time. I had to rehearse." Jessica held out her book, and Lila saw that it was a copy of *Macbeth*.

"It figures," said Lila. "Lately it seems as though that book's been surgically attached to your hand."

"Look across the hall," said Jessica suddenly. "There's that girl again—the one that's always staring at me lately."

Lila turned to see a thin, mousy-looking girl. The girl looked away quickly.

"I told you, I have no idea who she is," Lila said. "And from the looks of her, I'm sure I don't want to."

The girl's dull brown hair was pulled back into a limp ponytail. She wore a shapeless tan cardigan over an outdated jumper that, in Lila's opinion, was much too long. "Some people have no fashion sense," Lila added.

"Luckily," said Amy, "we've got more exciting things to talk about than her now that David Goodman is producing *Macbeth* here. Nothing interesting has happened in weeks—not since Dana Larson almost married Prince Arthur! Though I still can't believe a real prince would choose Dana with both of you falling all over him."

7

"If I can't be a real princess," Jessica declared, "at least I can play a queen!"

Lila turned to Amy. "How do you like that?" she asked. "Auditions don't even start until tomorrow, and Lady Wakefield is already behaving as though she has the lead all sewn up. If I were you, Jessica, I wouldn't bother memorizing too many of Lady Macbeth's lines—that is, unless you plan to understudy *me*. I'm going to get the role. And I'm sure Jessica can deal with her jealousy in a mature way."

"This play is the most important thing that's ever happened here," Jessica said, ignoring Lila's last comment. "And *nothing* is going to stop me from playing Lady Macbeth."

"Sam!" called Jessica, waving. "Over here!"

Sam pulled his car to a stop outside Sweet Valley High that afternoon. Jessica slid in next to him and then leaned over to give her boyfriend a kiss.

"How's my favorite actress?"

"Not so happy, yet much happier," said Jessica.

"Huh?" he asked, narrowing his gray eyes.

"It's from *Macbeth*," Jessica explained. "I mean I'm so excited about this play that I can hardly stand it. The part of Lady Macbeth was written for me. I know it was! But I'm also so nervous that I don't see how I'm going to get through the audition tomorrow."

"Just my luck," said Sam. "A date with the girl I love, and she can only think about some play."

"Some play?" Jessica cried. "Do you think that's all this is?"

"Come on, Jess," said Sam. "I was only teasing. I know how important this production is to you."

"Sorry," said Jessica. "I guess I did overreact. But Sam, this isn't really a date. Remember, I only have time for a soda at the Dairi Burger. Then I've got to get home to practice. I have to be a perfect Lady Macbeth by tomorrow afternoon."

"Don't worry," he reassured her. "You're going to be great. Nobody at Sweet Valley High could be a better Lady Macbeth than you. I just don't want you to forget your poor old boyfriend during your rapid rise to the top of the theatre world."

"Never!" Jessica said, gazing fondly at Sam. "Hey, you should've seen Elizabeth's face when I told her she could have the Jeep for a change. I thought she'd faint! Actually, she asked me to thank you. She had to stay after school to help Penny."

"Penny?" Sam asked.

"Penny Ayala. You've met her," Jessica reminded him. "The editor of *The Oracle*. She's tall and kind of boring."

A car horn sounded behind them, and Sam grinned. "Now, my queen," he said, "we'd better starteth the car and geteth out of the way. We blocketh traffic." He turned the key in the ignition and put the car in gear, then began to move into traffic.

"Wait!" Jessica yelled.

9

Sam slammed on the brakes. The car behind them honked again. "What is it, Jessica?"

She smiled sheepishly. "I'm sorry, Sam. I didn't mean to almost cause an accident. But I just saw that girl I told you about, the one who's been turning up everywhere I go." She pointed. "That's her standing near the doorway. She's the thin, mousy one with the messy hair."

Sam shook his head and started the car moving again. "She doesn't look as sinister as you've made her out to be, Jessica."

"I guess not," Jessica admitted. "It's just kind of creepy. She always seems to be *watching* me."

"No doubt she has some fiendish plan to murder you in your sleep while pretending to be your loyal friend and subject. She's Macbeth to your King Duncan."

"Very funny," said Jessica. "Now who can think of nothing but *Macbeth*?"

"I'm thinking of trying out for the play," said Annie Whitman at lunch the next day.

Jessica, Amy, and Lila were eating lunch in the crowded school cafeteria, and Annie pulled out a chair to join them.

"I don't want to discourage you, Annie," said Jessica, "but you ought to be more realistic. You don't have a chance at playing Lady Macbeth. Not with me trying out."

"And me!" said Lila.

Like Jessica and Amy, Annie was on the Sweet Valley High cheerleading squad. With her graceful figure and dark hair, Annie was pretty enough to be an actress, Jessica supposed. But when it came to playing royalty, she would be no match for flashy Jessica Wakefield or even elegant Lila Fowler. Besides, Annie was only a sophomore.

"Oh, I'd never dream of trying out for Lady Macbeth," said Annie, giggling. "Besides, you've got that in the bag, Jess."

Jessica smiled modestly at Annie and then cast a triumphant glare at Lila.

"I thought I'd try out for one of the smaller roles," Annie continued. "I've got a lot of time on my hands since Tony and I broke up." She blushed, but went on. "And my mother will be in New York on a modeling assignment for most of next month, so I would just end up sitting at home alone every night. The play will give me something to do with myself."

Jessica had noticed that Annie seemed down recently—ever since Tony Esteban had dumped her for another girl. *You'd never find me sitting at home alone because of some guy*, Jessica thought.

Amy's voice broke in on her thoughts. "Bill Chase is sure to get the part of Macbeth," she said. "He's the best actor at school. But won't that be uncomfortable for you, Jess?" She smiled wickedly at Jessica, and then glanced apologetically at Lila. "I mean, *if* you get the part of Lady Macbeth."

"She's right, Jessica," said Lila. "You were pretty rough on him when you both starred in *Splendor in the Grass*."

"Can I help it if he had a crush on me?" said Jessica innocently. "I allowed him to wait on me

11

hand and foot only because it made him so happy." She laughed. "Besides," she continued, "Bill *is* the best actor at school. I can't risk my big chance by co-starring with anyone else."

"Jessica!" Elizabeth called out over the lunchtime din. She waved, and then jostled her way through the crowd to her sister's table. Todd was right behind her.

"We can only stay a minute," began Elizabeth, out of breath. "But I've got the greatest news! Mr. Collins and Mr. Jaworski are the faculty advisors for the play, and you'll never believe who they just asked to be the student publicity director!"

"Let me guess," said Jessica. "Could it be Mr. Collins's star English student, Elizabeth Wakefield?"

"How did you know?" asked Elizabeth.

"Who else would they pick?" said Jessica. "Every teacher in school knows you're the most responsible, best-organized person at Sweet Valley High."

"You make *responsible* sound like a dirty word," said Todd.

"Sorry," Jessica said to her sister. "But I didn't mean it in a bad way." She thought for a moment and then grinned. "Actually, Liz, this is fantastic! You can make sure my picture is on all the posters!"

Todd rolled his eyes, and Elizabeth laughed. "Thanks for your selfless support," she said, hitting Jessica lightly on the head with her French textbook.

Jessica turned to grab the book. As she did she

noticed the same thin, mousy girl she had seen earlier. The girl was sitting alone at a nearby table and staring intently at Jessica and her friends.

"There's that girl we saw in the hall yesterday," Jessica said in a loud whisper. "And yesterday afternoon she was outside school when Sam picked me up. Every time I turn around, she's there."

"I've seen her, too," Elizabeth said. "I think she's a transfer sophomore."

"That's right," said Annie. "She just started here a few weeks ago. Her name's Paula Perrine. She's in my English class, but she mostly keeps to herself."

"It's getting weird," said Jessica. "Not only did I see her twice yesterday, but last week she was hanging around outside the gym after cheerleading practice. I think she must be following me."

"Aren't you being a little paranoid, Jessica?" asked Todd.

"I'm sure it's just a coincidence," Annie said quickly.

"Yeah," Jessica agreed, a little uncertainly. "It's probably just a coincidence." When her friends weren't looking, she glanced over at Paula Perrine again. This time, Paula didn't look away.

Two

"She's here!" Jessica whispered. "She's sitting way in back. I noticed her watching me while I auditioned." She slid into the seat Elizabeth had saved for her in the front row of the darkened auditorium.

Elizabeth turned and saw Paula Perrine sitting alone in the back row. "I know you're nervous about this audition, Jess, but Todd's right. You're starting to sound really paranoid about this girl. Calm down—you did a great job up there!" She gestured toward the stage and then squeezed her sister's shoulder supportively.

"Who do you think will play Banquo?" Elizabeth said, hoping to take Jessica's mind off her nervous delusions. "I liked Winston's reading—though it seems strange to think of him in a tragedy." Elizabeth's friend Winston Egbert was the unofficial clown of the junior class.

14

"That nerd?" Jessica asked. "Is he planning to try out?"

"You really are a basket case," said Elizabeth. "He just *did* try out, twenty minutes ago. And he's not a nerd," she added. "I've never seen you this nervous, Jess."

"Nervous? I'm not nervous!" Jessica's hair glistened like gold under the house lights as she twisted a few strands of it around her fingers. "Why should I be nervous? I'm the best person for the part. I know I am. Aren't I?"

"All you have to worry about today is making it through the first cuts," soothed Elizabeth. "And I'm sure you will. You were really good in the last scene you did with Bill, the one in which he was having second thoughts about the murder and you convinced him to go ahead with it."

Jessica whirled in her seat. "Only in that scene? What about the other scene I read? Oh no! I was terrible in that one, wasn't I? I read it too fast, didn't I? Tell me the truth."

Elizabeth sighed. Jessica's mood swings were getting tiresome. "You were great, Jessica," she said, a little tersely. "In both scenes."

"Why is Paula what's-her-name here?" demanded Jessica. "Why is she everywhere I go?"

"If you change the subject any faster, we'll both get whiplash," said Elizabeth. "Paula goes to school here, remember? She's got as much right to be here as we do."

"I guess you're right," said Jessica. She smiled, and changed the subject back to the auditions. "At least, I was tons better than Lila, wasn't I?"

15

She gestured to one side of the auditorium, where Lila was sitting with a tall, black-haired senior boy who had also tried out.

"Actually, Lila could have been a terrific Lady Macbeth—maybe as good as you. But she really fell apart in the audition. You worked a lot harder to prepare for it, and it showed."

Mr. Goodman stepped onto the stage. He was about the same age as the twins' parents, but had an unruly shock of prematurely white hair.

"Ladies and gentlemen," he began, "thank you for your time and effort." He tried to push aside the white hair that tumbled down over his eyes, but only managed to mess it up even more.

"As you know," he continued, "the roles we are casting first—which include most of the major characters—are for six males and five females. In this first round of cuts, I have narrowed the field to ten young men and ten young women."

Elizabeth watched Jessica's eyes follow the director's every move as he slowly pulled a sheet of paper from his breast pocket. She felt Jessica's hand on her arm as he read the names of the ten boys who had made the first cut. Naturally, Bill Chase was one of them. Elizabeth was glad to hear Winston's name as well.

Jessica's grip tightened as Mr. Goodman went on to the girls' names. Elizabeth hoped he would finish quickly; her sister's fingernails were digging painfully into her wrist.

"Patty Gilbert, Emily Mayer, Jean West, Joanne Shreves, Annie Whitman, Lila Fowler—" Mr.

Goodman stopped to clear his throat, and Elizabeth heard a sharp intake of breath from Jessica.

"Also Jennifer Morris, DeeDee Gordon, Rosa Jameson—and Jessica Wakefield."

Jessica's smile was electric in the dim room.

When the twins left the auditorium a few minutes later, Elizabeth was sure she saw Paula Perrine still watching Jessica intently. For once, Jessica was too excited to notice.

"I can't believe I made it! I just can't believe it!" exclaimed Jessica at the dinner table that night. "Yes, I can. I was the best, wasn't I, Liz? I'm going to be the best Lady Macbeth anyone has ever seen!"

"Is that the fourth time she's said that, or the fifth?" asked their brother, Steven, helping himself to some more spaghetti sauce. Like their father, he was tall and dark-haired. In fact, Jessica—an expert in such matters—often said he was the best-looking boy in town. But right now he was being his usual infuriating self.

"I have not said it five times!" she objected. "OK, maybe I have. But why do you come to dinner here, except to hear about my exciting life?"

Steven was a freshman at the nearby state university. He lived in a dormitory, but often dropped by his family's house to visit. Lately—ever since his girlfriend, Cara Walker, moved to London—he had been over several times a week. Jessica felt sorry for Steven. Cara had been one

17

of her closest friends; she missed her, too. But that was no excuse for not getting on with life.

Other people's problems seldom occupied Jessica's mind for long. She turned to her twin. "Have you decided what the posters for the play will look like? I think they should have a big closeup of me looking lovely and tragic!" She posed dramatically with the back of her hand against her forehead.

"Hold on, Lady Jessica," said Elizabeth. "I know how hard you're working for this, but you still have to make it through two more rounds of auditions. And I've got a much better idea for the posters: I'm holding a contest! The winning design will become the official poster. We'll put it up all around town, and on the play programs, too."

"Do you mean that somebody besides Jessica is involved in this production?" asked Mr. Wakefield. "I was beginning to think she was playing every role, designing the posters, directing the play, and cooking the witches' brew all by herself!"

"Are you certain you want to get your start with this particular play?" asked Steven. "In fact, both of you 'weird sisters' had better be careful." His voice sank to a whisper. "Have you heard about—*the Macbeth curse*?"

"Curse?" scoffed Jessica. "You're making it up."

"No, I'm not. Honest," said Steven. "I'm taking a Shakespeare class this term, and the professor keeps talking about this *Macbeth* thing. People in

18

the theatre world say it's an unlucky play. A lot of professional actors won't even say the word *Macbeth*. They call it 'the Scottish play' instead."

"How interesting," said Elizabeth. "But how can a play be unlucky?"

"Actually, Lady Macbeth was the first unlucky part of all," Steven began, looking at Jessica. "I bet you don't know who was the very first person to play Macbeth's wife."

"Katharine Hepburn?"

"Sorry, Jess," said Steven, smiling. "But it goes back a little further. In Shakespeare's time, women weren't allowed to be in plays, so men and boys played all the roles."

Jessica tried to imagine some bearded guy playing the beautiful Lady Macbeth, and couldn't. Steven must be teasing her, as usual. But Elizabeth and their parents were nodding as if they already knew that.

"The very first time the play was performed," Steven continued, "the boy who was going to play Lady Macbeth got sick at the last minute. So Shakespeare himself played the part."

"I didn't know that," said his mother.

"Oh, there's more. For hundreds of years, cast and crew members have died during performances of *Macbeth*—sometimes right onstage! My English lit professor's got dozens of stories." He turned to Jessica. "Are you sure you want this role, Jess? It could prove to be—" he bugged out his eyes—"hazardous to your health!"

"Very funny. Too bad we're not doing a comedy. You could play all the roles yourself!" said

Jessica, glaring at him. But she was a little uneasy. Could a play really be cursed?

"So what else are you doing for publicity, Elizabeth?" asked her father.

"I met with Mr. Collins and Mr. Jaworski about it today. The *Sweet Valley News* has agreed to publish an article about the play. I'll write that article, as well as some press releases. We're hoping that the *Los Angeles Times* and some of the other big newspapers will send reviewers on opening night. Maybe even *L.A. Arts* magazine."

"That's wonderful!" exclaimed Jessica. "My name will be all over the state! Elizabeth, do you think you can get them to run photographs of me, too?"

Steven laughed. "I hate to wrench the subject away from Jessica's admiring public, but I noticed a For Sale sign on the house next door. I didn't know the Beckwiths were moving."

"That's right," said his father. "The sign went up today. I spoke with Bob Beckwith; he's been transferred to Washington, D.C. It was pretty sudden, but he couldn't turn down the promotion. The catch is that they have to be there by the end of the month."

"I wonder who we'll get as new next-door neighbors," said Elizabeth.

"Maybe someone with a gorgeous teenage son," said Jessica.

"What happened to this Woodruff character you're supposed to be in love with?" asked Steven.

"Of course I'm in love with Sam!" Jessica replied. "I didn't say I want to date anyone else. But can't I still appreciate beauty when I see it?"

"That's all we guys are—decorations! You value us only for our pretty faces and tanned bodies."

"Exactly!" said Jessica and Elizabeth together.

"Well, Steven," said Jessica, jumping up, "as much as I'd like to stay here and admire *your* pretty face and tanned body, I have to get upstairs and memorize a scene for the audition tomorrow."

"Excuse me, Lady M.," began her father. "But don't you also have some French conjugations to memorize? I hear that Ms. Dalton is giving a test tomorrow."

"Some people have big mouths," said Jessica, glaring at Elizabeth. "Really, Daddy, all the teachers are being extra flexible about schoolwork for cast members."

"You're not a cast member yet, young lady," said her mother. "I know how important this play is to you, but I want you to spend some time with your French textbook before you pick up that script."

"Nobody understands a star," said Jessica with a sigh. "But yes, I will retire presently to my chamber, there to study mine own French verbs." She exited the dining room with a dramatic flourish. "Good night, sweet parents," she called from the stairs. "Parting is such sweet sorrow!"

"Yet do I fear thy nature," Jessica mused onstage Wednesday afternoon. "It is too full of the

21

milk of human kindness to catch the nearest way."

Absorbed in a dramatic monologue, Jessica as Lady Macbeth was contemplating the chances of her husband's going through with the murder. It was the last scene in that day's round of auditions. Afterward, Mr. Goodman and his assistants would decide which students to call back for a third audition.

The auditorium was dim, but it was easy to pick out Mr. Goodman, sitting in the middle of the room. His white hair bobbed slightly as he nodded to himself, and Jessica was sure he was smiling.

But she didn't need to see his reaction to know she was doing well. She could feel it. And the director had seemed impressed that she already knew some of Lady Macbeth's scenes. Thank goodness for Elizabeth, she thought. Without her coaching Sunday night, Jessica wouldn't have understood what all these lines meant.

"Not without ambition, but without the illness should attend it," she said thoughtfully, reflecting on Macbeth's weakness. *Illness means ruthlessness,* she translated to herself as she read. *My husband is ambitious—he wants to be king—but he's not rotten enough to think of the most effective way of getting there.*

Bill Chase joined her onstage a few minutes later, playing Macbeth. As soon as he began his lines Jessica forgot that he was reading from a script. *He really is good at this,* she thought. Despite Bill's "Surf Stop" T-shirt, she could almost believe that he was the Thane of Cawdor and she was his wife.

"He that's coming must be provided for," she told him aloud, "and you shall put this night's great business into my dispatch." As she said the words she was mentally translating them: "We have to be ready to deal with King Duncan when he gets here. Let me handle it."

For a moment, she was distracted by a sliver of light that expanded and then disappeared into the darkness in the back of the auditorium as a late arrival opened the door. The rectangle of light had shone for a few seconds on someone sitting alone in the back row. It was Paula Perrine.

Then Jessica heard her cue, spoke the last lines of the scene, and swept regally offstage ahead of Bill. For the first time since auditions had begun, she heard a smattering of applause.

Backstage, Bill turned to her. "Great work, Jessica!"

"Thanks, Bill," she said to the tall, blond surfer. "You were terrific, too! You're sure to get the lead. But wouldn't you rather have DeeDee play Lady Macbeth? After all, DeeDee is your girl-friend as well as president of the drama club."

Bill smiled. "Don't worry about DeeDee," he told her. "She has her heart set on playing Hecate, the witches' leader. Lady Macbeth is a pretty demanding part," he explained. "DeeDee's in charge of sets and scenery for this production; she wants to have the time to make them really great."

Jessica was relieved. She hadn't really considered DeeDee to be serious competition, but it was nice to know that her leading man wouldn't resent her for getting the part.

When Bill left, Jessica stood backstage by herself for a moment. She crossed her fingers for luck. "I have to get this part!" she whispered. Then she went out to join Elizabeth in the front row.

"I've never heard you do it so well!" her twin whispered as Jessica sat down.

"I really felt good up there, Liz, like everything was going absolutely, perfectly right. Steven's wrong about a curse. For me, *Macbeth* is a *lucky* play! I can't stand waiting to find out if I made it."

"Don't worry. I'm sure you'll make today's cuts," said Elizabeth. "But I forgot to tell you that I've got a publicity meeting right after these auditions. Can you catch a ride home with Lila?"

"Gee, Liz, I don't think so. I know it's your turn to have the Jeep, but Lila's going straight to the mall after this. She and Amy wanted me to come along, but I've got to get home right away to work on my scene for the final callback tomorrow." *If I make today's cut, that is!* she thought.

"All right," said Elizabeth. "I won't stand in the way of stardom. Todd's here late for basketball practice; I'll ask him for a lift home."

"Thanks, Liz. You're the greatest."

"Hi, Jessica. Hi, Elizabeth," called Amy, catching sight of the twins from the aisle. "Have you seen Lila? I'm supposed to meet her here."

"I think she's over there with some cute senior," said Jessica, pointing. But Lila had already noticed Amy's arrival and was heading toward them.

"Well?" Amy asked her a minute later, gesturing toward the guy she had been sitting with.

"His name's Tony Alimenti," said Lila with a frown. "I can't believe he had the nerve to ask me out! I mean, I've only talked to him a few times." Lila shook her head and took a seat next to Jessica. "Guys! Anyway, Mr. Goodman will be out any minute. I guess we might as well hear the news together."

The auditorium became silent as Mr. Goodman stepped onstage. "Ladies and gentlemen," he said, "it's time to narrow the field to six young men and five young women. All of those whose names I am about to call will be offered major roles in this production. In addition, some of the students whose names are not called today may be offered parts as understudies."

"Why can't he get on with it?" Jessica whispered.

Mr. Goodman pushed a lock of snowy hair out of his eyes. "Of course, you have all indicated the roles you prefer, but obviously we cannot cast every student as the character of his or her choice. The third and final audition, to be held Friday morning, will determine which role each student will play."

Jessica watched as he slowly unfolded a sheet of paper and began reading the boys' names. "Tom McKay, Bill Chase, Winston Egbert, Ted Jenson, Aaron Dallas, and Andy Jenkins."

"Now the girls," Jessica prompted under her breath. "Please, please pick me!"

She felt Elizabeth squeeze her hand.

"The following five girls will go on to the third round of auditions the day after tomorrow," he continued. Jessica held her breath as he read the list. "Annie Whitman, Lila Fowler, DeeDee Gordon, Rosa Jameson, and Jessica Wakefield."

Jessica squealed and jumped out of her seat. She hugged Elizabeth and then turned to face Lila.

"Congratulations, Lila," said Jessica. "I'm glad we both made it."

"Congratulations, Jessica," said Lila. "And may the best Lady Macbeth win. So how about changing your mind and coming to the mall with us? Lisette's is having a sale!"

For a moment Jessica was tempted. Lisette's was one of her favorite boutiques. But a great actress had to make sacrifices for her art. "No thanks," she said. "But you two have a good time."

As Amy and Lila walked toward the exit Jessica reminded herself that this play was the most important thing in the world. Still, she felt a little sad watching her friends laugh and talk as they moved away from her.

"Here are the keys to the Jeep," said Elizabeth.

26

"Thanks, Liz," said Jessica. "I've got just enough time to talk to Mr. Goodman before he gets tied up with that meeting of yours."

Giving the famous director an opportunity to meet her personally could only help her chances, Jessica reasoned. He was standing in the aisle, speaking to one of his assistants—a cute, muscular, blond guy who didn't look much older than Jessica. Probably some sort of college intern, she figured. Well, it couldn't hurt to make a good impression on him, too.

Ten minutes later, she pushed open the heavy side door of the auditorium. She was startled to see Paula Perrine standing outside. For a moment, Jessica felt an irrational fear at the sophomore's sudden presence. Then she gathered her wits and stared coldly at the skinny girl, who was wearing a faded plaid skirt and a clashing sweater.

"I've seen you watching me," Jessica said tersely.

"Oh, yes!" said Paula fervently. "I *have* been watching you. Who wouldn't? I think you're just great!"

Jessica had started to walk on, but now she stopped and turned. The girl was a little weird, but maybe she wasn't all bad.

"I know you'll get the part," Paula said quickly. "I love the theatre, and I can tell you're meant to be a star."

"Well, thanks," said Jessica. *Is this girl for real?*

27

Jessica thought. She started to walk across the parking lot, and Paula walked with her. "It's Paula Perrine, right?" Jessica asked.

"Oh, wow! I don't believe Jessica Wakefield actually knows my name!" cried Paula. Then she stopped, blushing. "I'm sorry. I didn't mean to embarrass you. It's just that you and your friends are so beautiful and so popular, I never dreamed you would notice someone like me."

"Hey, it's OK," said Jessica. "We may be popular, but we're not stuck-up—at least, some of us aren't," she added, thinking of Lila. "Well, this is my Jeep. I've gotta go. It was, uh, nice to meet you."

"Oh, the thrill is all mine, I swear," said Paula. "And Jessica, if there's anything I can do for you —anything—just let me know!"

As Jessica pulled away from the school she glanced into the rearview mirror. Paula was standing motionless in the parking lot, gazing at the Jeep as it moved away.

Three

"Eye of newt, and toe of frog, wool of bat, and tongue of dog!" exclaimed Winston, eyeing his lunch tray the next day. "I've been trying for years to figure out what they put into these barbecue sandwiches. Leave it to good old Will Shakespeare to provide the recipe."

Elizabeth laughed. "You're auditioning for the wrong part, Winston," she said. "Maybe you should play one of the witches."

"No way," objected Annie from the next table. "I've got enough competition as it is."

"That's true," remarked Lila. "Especially from Jessica. She's sure to be cast as a witch—she's a natural."

Uh-oh, thought Elizabeth. *Now we're going to see some real action.*

"Come on, you two," Amy cautioned. "Please don't fight about this play."

Jessica looked up from her script. "We're not fighting," she said calmly. "I told you all—I'm going to play Lady Macbeth. Wait and see." Elizabeth thought her twin's voice sounded strangely intense.

Lila laughed. "On second thought," she said, "playing a witch would be too easy for Jessica—typecasting, you know. Someday I should try that kind of role. With my beauty and disposition, it would be a real stretch. Of course, I'm a good enough actress to pull it off."

"Now *that* I'd like to see," said Amy's boyfriend, Barry Rork.

"Elizabeth, have you set up the rules for the poster contest?" Olivia Davidson asked. Olivia worked on *The Oracle* with Elizabeth and was known for her artistic talent. "I've got a lot of ideas."

"Fantastic!" said Elizabeth. "Mr. Goodman and his assistants will pick the winning poster. But I'd like to get people working together on this. You know, kind of a cooperative competition." She raised her voice and looked around at the entire group. "I'm planning an informal work session at my house Sunday afternoon. Everyone's invited! You'll be there, Todd, won't you?"

"Sure, Liz, if you want me to," Todd said. "But you know I can't even draw stick people."

"Me neither," said Elizabeth. "But if we've got a few artists around, like Olivia and DeeDee and David Prentiss, people like you and me and Enid might be able to help them come up with ideas."

"If nothing else, it's a great excuse to sit out

by your pool and work on our tans," said Enid, swiping a french fry from Elizabeth's tray.

"I, for one, would love to have an excuse to sit by the pool," said Annie. "My mother left this morning for that job in New York, so I've got a weekend alone to look forward to. And who knows? Maybe I'll come up with the winning poster idea!"

"It sounds pretty dull," said Lila. "But never fear, Jessica—Amy and I will rescue you from the attack of the artsy types. We haven't spent an afternoon at the beach in weeks. You've got to see the great bikini I found at Lisette's yesterday!"

"I'm not sure I can," said Jessica. "I think I'm doing something with Sam on Sunday."

"Did I hear you right?" said Amy. "The great actress has a life outside the theatre?"

"Actually, we were planning to rent the movie version of *Macbeth* and watch it at Sam's house."

"I never thought I'd say this to Jessica Wakefield, but lighten up!" said Winston. "Methinks the lady doth work too much."

"Certainly not on her classes," said Elizabeth. "Ms. Dalton said she'd have the French test back to us tomorrow, Jess. What are you going to tell Mom and Dad?"

"I may not have done *that* badly on the test," said Jessica. "Besides, what's more important, verb conjugations or a career in the theatre? I won't need to know French when I'm a famous actress!"

Jessica looked up, away from the table, and nodded slightly. Elizabeth followed her sister's glance and saw Paula standing a few steps away, listening. Nobody else seemed to have noticed her.

"Oh, no." Todd groaned. "Not Lady Wakefield's famous-actress routine again."

"Why not?" asked Jessica. "I'm going to get this part, and I'm going to be the best Lady Macbeth that Mr. Goodman has ever seen!"

Just then Paula stepped closer, and Jessica finally acknowledged her.

"Hi, Paula," she said. "Do you know everyone?"

"Oh yes," said Paula, almost in a whisper. "Everyone knows who *all of you* are." Elizabeth thought she had never seen anyone so shy—or so overawed by Jessica and her friends.

Jessica looked expectantly at the thin girl, obviously waiting for her to get to the point.

Sometimes her twin could be so insensitive, Elizabeth thought. "Would you like to join us, Paula?" she asked, ignoring a dirty look from Lila. "There's an extra chair."

"Oh, no," said Paula. "Thank you, but I couldn't possibly. I just wanted to ask Jessica . . . I mean, I know you'll get the part anyway, but if you'd like, I could go over your lines with you before the last audition tomorrow. I mean, if you want me to."

Lila rolled her eyes, but Jessica smiled graciously.

"Thanks, Paula. That would be great," she said.

Paula smiled shyly.

"Seriously, I could use some help," Jessica continued, throwing a pointed glance at Elizabeth. "My sister has been much too busy writing her newspaper stories to be of much assistance lately. How about if we get together after school today?"

"I'd love you to come to my house—" began Paula. Then she stopped suddenly and blushed. "But we're remodeling the living room, and it's kind of a mess."

"That's OK," said Jessica. "We can do it at my house. How about four o'clock?" She gave her the address.

Paula smiled broadly. Then she gave Jessica an embarrassed wave and hurried away.

"Wow," said Enid. "She's really shy."

"Did you see that getup she was wearing? Polyester—ugh!" Lila scoffed. "She has absolutely no taste."

"You're just jealous because she thinks *I'd* make the best Lady Macbeth," said Jessica.

"As I said," Lila retorted, "she has no taste. No taste whatsoever."

"Tomorrow's the big day!" Jessica said into the phone that night.

"I'd almost forgotten," said Sam. "It's the regional chess club tournament, right?"

"You creep! You know very well that tomorrow morning is the last round of auditions for *Macbeth*. Teachers are even letting us miss class for it."

Sam laughed. "Of course I know! It's the only thing you've talked about all week. And tomor-

33

row after school this famous director of yours will announce the cast list—which will include a certain blond knockout as Lady Macbeth."

"Do you really think so?"

"You've got it in the bag—and you know it!"

"Sometimes I think so," Jessica admitted. "But then I get scared. What if this play is so unlucky that I don't get the part? I told you what Steven said about a curse."

"Don't tell me you're worried about that superstitious garbage."

"No, not really," said Jessica with a laugh. "I'm just so nervous, it's turning me into a space cadet."

"I'll say!" said Sam. "When I picked you up Monday afternoon, you were really going off the deep end about that girl you saw outside school. What did she turn out to be—a secret agent or a terrorist?"

"OK already!" Jessica laughed. "I admit it. I was completely wrong about Paula. She was only watching me because she wanted to be my friend. In fact, she came over after school today and helped me practice my lines."

"Good," said Sam. "I'm glad you're not spooked about her anymore."

"You know," Jessica mused, "it's nice having someone around who only wants to make me happy. Paula is so sweet and generous—she does anything I ask her to do, and is cheerful about it. Lila and Amy always have ulterior motives. Paula really looks up to me. And she thinks I have a great chance at playing Lady Macbeth."

"She's not the only one," said Sam. "In fact,

there's a certain dirt bike racer who already thinks of you as a queen."

Jessica bit her lip and thought for a minute. "Seriously, Sam," she said, "I want this part more than anything I've ever wanted in my life. This is my chance to be discovered as an actress. I'll just die if I don't get to be Lady Macbeth!"

"Over here, Paula!" Annie called out in the school cafeteria the next day. She gestured to a chair. "Sit with me and Lila and Amy."

"Oh, I couldn't," Paula stammered. "I'd be imposing."

"Well, if you insist," Lila began, eyeing Paula's out-of-style pantsuit. Whatever Annie and Jessica thought of Paula, Lila Fowler was not into charity cases.

"Of course you're not imposing," Annie assured the new girl.

"I'm surprised that you're not with your better half today, Paula," began Lila. "Jessica said she had to rehearse during lunch. She's hardly spoken to *me* all week, but I figured *you'd* be helping her practice her lines again."

"Oh, I offered to," explained Paula, "but Jessica and Bill Chase wanted to work on a scene together."

"I don't get it," Amy objected. "The final round of auditions was this morning and the cast won't be announced until after school today. It's too late to rehearse for tryouts, and too early to rehearse for performances. So why are they rehearsing?"

"A real artist never stops perfecting her art," said Paula.

"So what's Jessica's excuse?" Lila joked.

"You have such a terrific sense of humor, Lila," said Paula. "If I didn't know how kind and understanding you are, I would almost think you were serious. But you know as well as I do just how dedicated an actress Jessica is."

"If you ask me, she's a dedicated pain in the neck," said Amy. "We were supposed to go shopping again last night. But once more, Lady Wakefield didn't show up. She told me this morning that rehearsing for the last audition was more important. I don't know why I even bother to make plans with her anymore."

"That's for sure," Lila complained. "She's been even more unreliable than usual—not to mention impossible to talk to. Paula, you're about the only one who's seen her outside of school lately. In fact, in the last two days, you seem to have become her shadow. I don't know how you put up with her!"

"I don't mind," Paula said with a quiet smile. "I'm just glad to be her friend. Jessica is so talented. And she wants this role so much."

"It's too bad she's got competition for it," Lila remarked icily.

"You know, Lila," said Paula, "Jessica is a very sensitive actress, but I've seen your auditions and I think you've got more range than she does. Maybe you should consider one of the more difficult roles in the play."

"I don't know," said Lila. "I might. But what

about you? You seem so interested in the theatre. Why aren't you trying out?"

"For me, it's enough just to be *close* to the theatre," Paula explained fervently. She stopped for a few seconds before continuing in a low voice. "When I was a little girl, my family moved around a lot, so I never had many friends." She looked down at her hands. "My parents used to fight all the time. The only way to escape was to pretend I was someone else. For hours, I'd make believe I was in my own magical world. I'd pretend I was a powerful queen or a beautiful genie."

Paula looked up and smiled wistfully. Her gray eyes were shining and she seemed to forget the noisy lunchroom around her. Normally, Lila wasn't interested in people who went on about themselves like this. But Paula was different. She seemed so sad and so sincere.

"The first time I saw a play," Paula continued, "it was like a dream come true! I started going to the theatre every chance I got. I would beg my mother to take me—" She stopped, blushing. "I'm sorry," she said. "I'm talking too much. I shouldn't be boring you like this."

"You're not boring us," Amy said. "Please go on."

"There isn't much more to tell," Paula said. "But ever since I saw that first play, I've always thought that the theatre was the most wonderful thing in the world!" She laughed nervously. "But I couldn't possibly get up onstage in front of so many people. I would never have the courage."

"Speaking of courage, has anyone tried this brown stuff?" asked Amy, pointing to something on her lunch tray. "I can't even figure out what it is."

"I think it's supposed to be peanut butter pudding," said Annie, grimacing.

"Here, Amy," said Paula, holding out a plastic bag. "I brought these chocolate chip cookies in my lunch, but I can't eat another thing. You take them."

"Thanks, Paula. That's nice of you."

"Lila, would you mind doing me a favor?" asked Paula.

"That depends on what it is," said Lila. Her tone was guarded but not unkind. Lila Fowler wasn't in the habit of doing favors for people she didn't know well—especially people who dressed like Paula. But oddly enough, she was beginning to feel somewhat protective toward the younger girl.

"Everyone says you're a terrific tennis player, Lila," Paula told her. "I could really use some pointers on my serve. If you're not busy tomorrow morning, I thought maybe we could play together."

Lila smiled. "You've come to the right place," she replied, swinging an imaginary racket. "I *am* a terrific tennis player. And I'd be happy to show you how it's done."

"Let's make it doubles!" said Amy. "Barry just helped me pick out a new racket, and I'm dying to try it out. How about it, Annie?"

"Oh, I don't know." Annie hesitated. "I'm not very good. Maybe you ought to ask Jessica instead."

"Of course I'd love to play tennis with Jessica," said Paula. "But you know how busy her schedule is. I'm rehearsing with her in the afternoon, but she'll be going over her lines by herself all morning."

"You're probably right," said Lila. "And even if we did get her to come, she'd spend the whole time talking about the play. She was a lot more fun before she decided to be a famous actress." She yawned. "The four of us will have a better time without her. Are you coming, Annie?"

"OK, you've convinced me," said Annie. "How about ten o'clock?"

"If you don't mind, I'd rather make it ten-thirty," Paula said. "I promised Jessica I'd have photocopies made of pages from a few of her scenes. I've got to stop by the copy shop in the morning to pick them up."

"Do you mean to say that she's got you running her errands, too?" Annie asked.

"Oh, I don't mind doing things for Jessica," Paula said earnestly. "I'm just glad to help her prepare for this play. It's the closest I'll ever get to being part of the theatre world."

Paula is certainly no judge of character, thought Lila. In fact, when it came to Jessica Wakefield, Paula sounded absolutely pathetic. But she really was sweet—especially when Jessica wasn't around.

*   *   *

"Hurry up, Chrome Dome," pleaded Jessica in a whisper. "I can't wait another minute!" School was out for the day, but Jessica was sitting in the auditorium with Paula, Lila, and Amy. They were waiting for the principal, Mr. Cooper, to announce who had won the most coveted roles in *Macbeth*.

Unfortunately, they first had to sit through one of Chrome Dome Cooper's long, boring speeches.

Finally, the principal seemed to be wrapping things up. "Now, without further ado," he announced, "I'd like to introduce a person who is going to be very important to everyone involved in this play . . ."

"Finally," whispered Jessica. "David Goodman."

"Elizabeth Wakefield!"

Jessica slumped down in her chair as Elizabeth began explaining the rules of the poster contest. Here she was, waiting for the most important, the most vital, the most critical announcement of her life, and Mr. Cooper was letting her own sister ramble on instead of introducing the famous theatre director.

Paula patted her on the shoulder and whispered, "Don't worry, Jessica. I'm sure you'll get the part. You were as wonderful as ever this morning in the final audition."

Jessica smiled gratefully. At least Paula was on her side.

Onstage, Elizabeth was coming to the end of her speech. "Feel free to come to me with any ideas you have for publicizing this play," she

40

said. "This is going to be the best production Sweet Valley High has ever put on. Let's do whatever we can to make sure everyone in Sweet Valley knows about it!"

Jessica clapped dutifully and checked to make sure her friends did, too. After all, Elizabeth *was* her sister. But she froze as soon as David Goodman appeared onstage. She held her breath while he adjusted the microphone.

"Ladies and gentlemen," the director began, "I have seen some outstanding student talent this week during the auditions for *Macbeth*. First, I'd like to thank everyone who tried out, as well as English teacher Roger Collins and dramatics teacher Don Jaworski for their invaluable assistance. And this young lady"—he gestured toward Elizabeth, who was sitting behind him on the stage—"Elizabeth Wakefield, publicity director, for her creativity and hard work."

Jessica wanted to stand up and scream at him to get on with it. Instead, she exhaled noisily and crossed her arms.

"If Ms. Wakefield's efforts are indicative of the attitude of all Sweet Valley students, then we shall have a most memorable production indeed."

He adjusted the microphone again. "But I know you're all waiting to hear who will make up the cast of *Macbeth*."

"No kidding!" Jessica whispered.

Mr. Goodman began reading from a clipboard. "The part of Malcolm will be played by Ted Jenson," he said. "Macduff will be played by Andy Jenkins. Aaron Dallas will play Lennox, and Tom

McKay will play Ross. Banquo will be played by Winston Egbert. And Macbeth himself will be portrayed by Bill Chase."

Mr. Goodman paused. Then he ran his fingers through his hair and lifted his clipboard again. Jessica sat up straight in her chair.

"The part of Hecate will be played by DeeDee Gordon. The three weird sisters will be portrayed by Annie Whitman, Rosa Jameson, and Lila Fowler. And the part of Lady Macbeth will be played by Jessica Wakefield."

"Yes!" screamed Jessica.

"No!" screamed Lila.

Mr. Goodman looked up at the interruption, but went on. "In addition," he said, "Josh Bowen will understudy the part of Macbeth, and Jennifer Morris will understudy Ms. Wakefield's Lady Macbeth. Other understudies as well as additional roles will be cast next week."

Mr. Cooper started to dismiss the assembly, but there was no need. The noise level rose as everyone stood up and began to comment excitedly on the cast announcements.

"Congratulations, Lady Wakefield!" said Winston, turning in his seat. He stood and bowed to Jessica.

"Thank you, my loyal subject," said Jessica.

"You know, Lila," Winston began in an academic tone, "the witches' roles present some of the most interesting dramatic challenges in *Macbeth*."

"I certainly don't care. I'll drop out of the production before I agree to play a witch!"

Amy winked at Winston and Maria behind Lila's back. "I think Winston's right, Lila. As you said the other day, it will be a real stretch, but you're a good enough actress to pull it off. You should accept the part. I can't think of a better way to showcase your talents."

Lila appeared to be softening. "I don't know. I guess I could *think* about it."

Jessica barely heard her friends. She had earned the part. She really was going to play Lady Macbeth. She was on her way to Broadway!

"Lila and I were planning to go to the mall for an ice cream at Casey's," Amy said. "Who wants to come along—Jessica? Paula?"

"I can't go," said Jessica. "I got a C-minus on that stupid French test. My parents made me promise to study for an hour before dinner tonight if I didn't get at least a C." She shrugged. "As if I had nothing better to do!"

But she was glad that Amy's invitation had included Paula. "Go with them, Paula," she urged. "It will be fun—even without me there."

"No, I really couldn't, but thank you all for inviting me," Paula said. "It means so much to me. But I've got to get home to study for a math test. Jessica, is seven-thirty all right for rehearsing at your house tonight?"

"Perfect!" said Jessica.

"And Jessica, congratulations on getting the part," Paula said, smiling sweetly. "I feel like I'm learning so much about acting just from watching you!"

Four

"Out, damned spot," Elizabeth said aloud that evening as she scrubbed a stir-fry pan at the kitchen sink. "Oh no," she groaned. "Now *I'm* corrupting Shakespeare, too!"

It was her sister's turn to wash the dishes but, as usual, Elizabeth was stuck with the chore. Jessica had insisted that she had to work on her lines. Now her twin was rehearsing in the den with Paula. Elizabeth could hear their voices above the rush of water running in the sink.

"We will proceed no further in this business," said Paula, reading the part of Macbeth.

She's not bad, thought Elizabeth, setting the wet pan down on the counter. The phone rang, and Elizabeth heard her mother's footsteps upstairs.

"Was the hope drunk wherein you dressed yourself?" demanded Jessica as Lady Macbeth.

44

"Hath it slept since? And wakes it now, to look so green and pale at what it did so freely?"

"Jessica!" called Mrs. Wakefield. "Sam's on the phone."

"Thanks, Mom. I'll take it in the living room. Sorry, Paula. I'll be back in a minute."

Elizabeth picked up a knife and swished it in the soapy water. From the living room, she could hear Jessica talking and giggling into the phone.

Elizabeth checked the time. Sometimes her sister could be incredibly rude. Paula had come to help her. Jessica had no right to leave her friend sitting by herself while she gabbed away with Sam. Well, somebody ought to be hospitable. Elizabeth dried her hands. She grabbed two root beers from the refrigerator, put some cookies on a tray, and headed toward the den. Prince Albert, the Wakefield's golden Labrador, followed her.

Elizabeth stopped at the doorway to the den, entranced. Paula stood alone in the middle of the room. The shy, awkward girl was gone. In her place was Lady Macbeth—dignified, majestic, and ruthless. In a whisper, Paula was reading from the script and gesturing with her free hand.

"And fill me, from the crown to the toe, top-full of direst cruelty!" Paula commanded the spirits. She spoke very quietly, but her reading carried such power that Elizabeth was mesmerized.

Then Paula looked up and saw her, and the spell was broken. She blushed and slammed the script shut.

"I'm sorry if I startled you, Paula," said Elizabeth kindly. "I didn't mean to interrupt."

45

"It's OK," Paula said. "You're not interrupting. I was just being silly. I'll never be as great an actress as your sister."

Elizabeth set down the tray and offered her a soda. "Don't sell yourself short," she said. "You sounded wonderful a minute ago."

"Oh, I'm just copying Jessica. She's perfect in every way! And I can't believe how nice she's being to me."

"Nice? If you ask me, it was pretty rude of her to leave you by yourself while she talks to her boyfriend," Elizabeth said with a chuckle.

"I don't mind, Elizabeth," said Paula earnestly. "I know how much she loves Sam. And she's had so little time to spend with him this week, what with the auditions for the play. Elizabeth, your sister is just incredible. I don't know what someone so wonderful sees in a nothing like me."

"Paula, there's no reason to put yourself down like that," Elizabeth said gently, sitting next to the younger girl.

"Tell me more about Jessica," Paula urged. "What's she really like? I mean, what would it be like to be her friend?"

"Well, she's been a little different lately, because she's so intent on this play," Elizabeth admitted. "But normally, Jessica is lively and outrageous and a lot of fun to be around. Of course, her friends wouldn't always agree with that last statement." She stopped, smiling.

"Some people consider Jessica to be, well, unreliable," she continued. Then Elizabeth turned serious. "But Paula, when the going gets rough,

Jessica is the most loyal person you could ever hope to meet."

"I thought so." Paula looked at her hands for a minute. "I bet Sam is great, too," she said suddenly. "Tell me about him."

"Actually, he's a lot like Jessica," Elizabeth said. "He's got a great sense of humor, and he really knows how to have a good time." She laughed. "He's also into dirt bike racing."

"Dirt bike racing? Does Jessica like that, too?"

"I think Jessica would prefer a cleaner sport. But she humors him." Elizabeth held out the plate of cookies. "No, Prince Albert! None for you!" she said, shooing away the dog. He padded over to the unfamiliar girl and sniffed at her. Paula drew back, frightened.

"Don't worry about Prince Albert," said Elizabeth, pulling him away and settling him on the rug, away from Paula. "He gets a little too friendly at times, but he wouldn't hurt a fly."

"I'm sorry," said Paula. "I know it's silly to be afraid of him. I don't mean to be such a baby. It's just that I've never had a dog."

"So," said Elizabeth, smiling at her, "you're a sophomore, you like the theatre, and you don't like dogs. It's a start. Tell me more about yourself, Paula."

"There's not much to tell," Paula said, shy again.

"What about your family?" Elizabeth encouraged her. "Jessica has probably told you that we have an older brother. Do you have any brothers or sisters?"

Paula turned away for a moment, and Elizabeth was afraid she was going to cry.

"I'm sorry, Paula," Elizabeth said quietly. "I didn't mean to pry. But if it would help to talk to somebody . . ."

"You're so nice," said Paula. "But I should have expected that from Jessica's sister." She quickly rubbed a hand across her eyes and continued. "I have an older brother, too, but he ran away from home a few months ago. We were living a couple of hours up the coast then."

Elizabeth's heart went out to the girl. "That's rough," she said. "Were you two very close?"

"Yes," said Paula. "And when he took off, he left me all alone with my father."

"Your parents are divorced?"

Paula blinked a few times. "My mother died last year," she said in a quiet, steady voice. "My father can be . . . well, abusive. He drinks too much. When my brother was home, it wasn't too bad. But after I was left alone with my father . . ." Paula's voice broke, and tears welled up in her eyes.

Elizabeth felt like crying, too. She gently laid a hand on Paula's arm. "I'm so sorry. I wish I could help. Is there anywhere else you can stay?"

"Everything's OK now," said Paula, dabbing at her eyes. "That's why I came to Sweet Valley. My mother had friends here; I'm living with them." She smiled. "Really, Elizabeth, I'm fine. And you don't know what it means to me to be here in your house with your family."

Poor Paula! No wonder she seemed so shy and

48

so alone. Now her attachment to Jessica was beginning to make sense to Elizabeth. *It must make her feel better to be around someone who's so full of life*, she thought. But Jessica tended to get carried away. She could easily take advantage of Paula's admiration. Elizabeth made a silent vow to watch out for Jessica's new friend.

Two hours later, Jessica was rehearsing alone in her room when Elizabeth came in, "Jess, can I talk to you for a few minutes?" she asked.

"Actually, Liz, I'm pretty busy right now," said Jessica, holding up her script. "Can we talk tomorrow? Paula and I got a lot done tonight, but I wanted to go over this monologue by myself a few more times. Rehearsals start Monday."

Elizabeth took the script from her and set it aside. "It's Paula that I want to talk to you about —and it can't wait." She moved a stack of papers from Jessica's desk chair and sat down. "Has she told you much about her family?"

"Why would we want to talk about her family?" asked Jessica. "I told you, rehearsals start Monday. We have to concentrate on the *play*."

"Jessica, did you know that her mother died last year?"

"Gee, Liz, she never told me. Poor kid. Hey, but why would she tell that to you? I'm her friend."

"I don't know, Jessica," Elizabeth said. "But she really admires you. Maybe she was embarrassed to have you know about her family problems."

49

"What's so embarrassing about her mother dying?"

"Jess, it gets worse," Elizabeth said gently. "Her father is an alcoholic. He used to drink and get abusive toward Paula and her older brother. She said that as long as her brother was there to protect her, it wasn't too bad."

"So what happened to her brother?" asked Jessica, horrified.

"He ran away from home a couple of months ago. Paula couldn't handle her father by herself, so she left, too. She came here to Sweet Valley to live with some friends of her mother."

"Oh, Liz!" cried Jessica. "How awful! I had no idea she'd been through all that. She never said a word!"

"I know," said Elizabeth. "Actually, I wasn't sure I should tell you. I know the other kids are beginning to like her, too, but you're still closer to her than anyone. You may be able to help her. Besides, I got the feeling that she *wanted* me to tell you."

"I still don't understand why she didn't tell me herself."

"Don't be too hard on her, Jessica. I think she just didn't know how to broach the subject. But you really could be nicer to her. I can't believe you left her alone in the den all that time while you were on the phone. After all, she was here to help you."

"You're right, Liz. The time just got away from me. But it won't happen again," she vowed. "From now on, I'm going to do everything I can to show Paula how welcome she is in Sweet Valley."

Through the sliding glass door, Jessica could see that the weather was perfect, as usual.

She sighed and resigned herself to staying indoors on a beautiful Saturday afternoon. She knew she would never get this scene right if she and Paula were outside, being distracted by the sunlight that sparkled on the water in the swimming pool. Still, maybe it was time to put Shakespeare aside for a few minutes.

"Let's take a break, Paula," she said, tossing her script onto the table. "I want to talk to you." She sat down and motioned for Paula to sit next to her. "Liz told me about your, uh, family situation. You know, you could have told me yourself, Paula. I'm your friend."

"I was afraid to, Jessica," said Paula, so quietly that Jessica had to strain to hear her. "I was afraid you wouldn't want me here if you knew."

"Of course I would," said Jessica. "You can count on me. I'll be there for you."

"Thank you, Jessica," Paula said fervently. "You and your sister have been so sweet to me. I don't deserve it."

"Of course you deserve it," said Jessica. "Look, you've got to get some self-confidence!" She thought for a moment. "You know, I've been listening to you read lines with me all week, and you're not bad—for a beginner, that is. You say you love the theatre. Why don't you try out for one of the smaller roles?"

"Try out for the play?" Paula asked, her eyes wide. "I could never do that!"

"Why not?" asked Jessica. "I'll put in a good word with Mr. Goodman for you."

"You would do that for me?"

"Of course I would."

Jessica picked up the script and scrutinized the character list. "I've got it! You can play the part of the gentlewoman; you'd be my lady-in-waiting. It's perfect. It's just one scene, with only a few lines to learn—and we'd be onstage together."

"Do you really think I could?" asked Paula. Then she hastily answered herself. "No, I couldn't. I'd be too scared even to try out. Actresses are supposed to be beautiful and poised—like you."

"That's true," Jessica conceded. "But I'll help you. A few fashion tips and a new hairstyle can work wonders. And I've got a shampoo that'll make your hair shine like satin." She jumped up from the couch. "Come upstairs now, and we'll get to work on you!"

An hour later, the girls gazed at a new Paula in the full-length mirror in Jessica's bedroom.

"Wow!" breathed Paula. "I can hardly believe it's me!"

"I'm even better at this than I thought," said Jessica with a giggle. "I never would have guessed that your hair had such pretty highlights."

"I always thought of it as plain old mousy brown," admitted Paula. "And you were right about the clothes. They do make me look a little less skinny."

"Do you think you'll be able to do the makeup yourself?" Jessica asked. "Remember, buy Peach Fizz blusher, dark brown mascara, and that sort of peachy-colored lipstick—the cream kind, not the frosted kind. And blend your eye shadow like I showed you."

"I couldn't possibly wear all this makeup to school, Jessica," Paula objected. "I'd be too embarrassed."

"But that's the whole idea!" Jessica pointed to Paula's reflection in the mirror. "Look at yourself. Does that look like a girl who's afraid of her own shadow?"

"No, I guess not," said Paula, smiling. "OK, I'll try. But let me do it gradually—just the new hairstyle at first. Then I'll add a little lipstick or something a few days later."

"I guess that's all right, if it makes you feel more comfortable," Jessica agreed. "But Paula, you don't have to feel guilty about looking great."

"I guess I'm afraid people will think I'm pretending to be something I'm not." Paula frowned and looked down at the borrowed vest.

"Nonsense," said Jessica. "Don't be so worried. Everyone at school is beginning to find out exactly who you are—a sweet and generous person."

Paula impulsively threw her arms around her. "Thank you for everything, Jessica," she said. "You're the best friend I ever had!"

Five

"What did Lady Macbeth say as she put out her dog?" Enid asked the students who were gathered around the Wakefield's pool the next day.

"Out, damned Spot!" Winston cried gleefully.

Elizabeth groaned. "If you keep this up, Banquo, everyone at school will want to play one of the three murderers who get to come after you."

"What can I say?" said Winston. "I'm a popular guy."

"OK, everyone," said DeeDee, "I've got a rough layout finished. I need some constructive criticism." She held up her sketchbook, and several people crowded around.

Elizabeth was impressed. "That's terrific, DeeDee."

"I really like the way you've drawn the expression on Macbeth's face," said Robin Wilson, pointing to a large closeup of Bill Chase in costume. "With just a few lines, you've managed to make him look power-hungry and tormented at the same time."

"She's right," said Olivia. "The drawing is excellent—simple, but expressive. But I think you need to add something small down at the bottom, to balance the composition. Maybe another figure?"

"Hmm," said DeeDee. "You know, you're right. But what should I put there?"

"A witch?" suggested Annie.

"How about a simple little silhouette of Shakespeare himself?" Robin asked.

"That just might work," said DeeDee. She picked up the sketchbook and began to draw it in.

"Hi there," Paula called, stepping through the sliding glass doors onto the patio. "I hope I'm not intruding."

"Of course not, Paula," Elizabeth said. "Jessica's up in her room rehearsing. But I've got to warn you—she's going over to Sam's house pretty soon." She put her hands on her hips. "It would be just like Jessica to invite you over to rehearse together and forget that she'd already made plans with Sam. She's been so distracted lately."

Paula smiled. "Oh, we didn't have plans to practice today. In fact, I figured she would already be gone. I really dropped by to see all of you—that is, if you don't mind."

"Mind?" Annie said. "I think it's great that

you've come over." She tugged an empty chair over next to hers. "You can help me critique all these people with real artistic talent—or are you an artist, too?"

"Not me!" Paula said, laughing. "I have no talent in anything whatsoever." She sat down next to Annie and pulled a small box out of her purse. "Actually, I was hoping you'd be here, Annie. I have a present for you."

"For me?" asked Annie. She took the box and turned it over in her hands. "But it's not my birthday."

"What's the occasion?" asked Robin.

"No occasion," said Paula, smiling shyly. "I just wanted to, that's all."

Annie opened the box and pulled out a brightly colored woven headband. "It's beautiful, Paula. But I can't accept it."

"Of course you can," said Paula. "It's really no big deal. It was a present from my grandmother last year, but the colors are hideous on me. I thought they would look pretty with your dark hair."

"She's right, Annie," said Olivia. "Bright colors are smashing on you. Try it on." She pulled a small mirror out of her bag and handed it to Annie.

Annie slipped on the headband and smiled at her reflection in the mirror. "Thank you, Paula," she said. "It was nice of you to think of me."

"I thought you didn't have any relatives except for your father, Paula," Robin said. "Isn't that why you're living with friends here in Sweet Valley?"

"I don't have any other relatives," Paula murmured, blushing. "Well, not really. I mean, the headband is from my grandmother on my father's side, so I couldn't run away from him to go live with *her*. She always sends a present on my birthday." Her voice grew softer and she looked down at her hands. "Aside from that, I haven't heard from her in years."

"I'm sorry, Paula," said Robin. "I know it's not very pleasant for you, talking about your family."

"Oh, it's OK," said Paula quietly. "Friends should share things with each other." She looked up at them all. "And I'm so glad to have all of you as friends."

"So share away!" said David Prentiss, holding up his sketchbook. "What does everyone think of this design?"

Elizabeth and Todd stepped inside a few minutes later to get everyone some snacks. Todd opened the refrigerator and pulled out the bowl of dip Elizabeth had made that morning.

"Paula Perrine seems like a very thoughtful girl," he said. "But she sure is shy."

"You're right on both counts," Elizabeth agreed. "I'm really beginning to like her. And I'm glad to see that she's starting to come out of her shell and make some more friends. She's much too dependent on Jessica." She handed him a tray. "Would you get some sodas and juice out of the refrigerator?"

"Yes, my queen," he said, bowing. "Your wish is my command."

"Did you notice David's poster design?" Elizabeth asked a moment later. "He's got to be one of the most artistic students at school. His *Macbeth* design is nearly as striking as the poster he did for the dance show earlier this year."

"He *is* awfully good," Todd agreed. "But I can't say that I think much of his taste in subjects! Jessica doesn't need the encouragement."

"Believe it or not, I'm *glad* that he's centering his design around Jessica as Lady Macbeth," said Elizabeth. "She's driving me crazy, bugging me about whether she's in any of the poster ideas. I'll never hear the end of it if one of the others is the winner."

"We're not interrupting anything, are we?" asked Robin, coming into the kitchen.

"Do you two need any help with the snacks?" Paula asked, walking in behind Robin.

"Sure! You can take out the potato chips."

"No problem," said Paula, reaching for the bag.

"Elizabeth, did I hear you say that Jessica is around?" Robin asked. "I really need to talk to her. I don't know how someone as responsible as you can be related to Jessica. She hasn't shown up for cheerleading practice in ages. Our being co-captains of the varsity squad means that we're *both* supposed to be there!"

"Be patient with her," Paula urged quietly. "Jessica's under a lot of stress right now."

"Paula's right. If I were you, Robin, I wouldn't interrupt my sister while she's rehearsing," Elizabeth warned. "She'll bite your head off! But don't worry—she said she'd drop by the pool to say hi before she goes over to Sam's. She'll be down soon."

Elizabeth was talking to Annie and Paula near the edge of the pool when Jessica finally made her entrance.

Jessica was halfway across the patio to them when she stopped suddenly. "Paula!" she said loudly. "I didn't know you were here."

"Is that OK, Jessica?" Paula asked sweetly.

"Of course," Jessica answered. "I was just surprised."

"Hi, Jess," said Annie. "We missed you at the special cheerleading practice today. Robin's been looking for you."

"Thanks for the warning," said Jessica with a scowl. "Maybe if I slip out now, she won't notice me."

"Too late," said Elizabeth. "She's coming this way. And Robin does have a point, Jessica. You could have at least called to tell her you wouldn't be there."

"You could've talked to *me* about it, Jessica," Paula said eagerly. "I know how busy you are these days. I could make phone calls for you—to take care of canceling appointments and things like that."

Jessica gave Paula a curious look.

"Jessica! Where were you this morning?" Robin demanded as she headed over to them. "Don't answer that. I know where you were. You were

59

too busy playing the queen to stoop to something as low-class as cheerleading. As long as you're co-captain of the squad, you have responsibilities. You promised to teach me that new cheer today."

"I know, Robin," said Jessica. "But this play is more important. Actually, I don't think I'll be coming to cheerleading practice at all until the play is over."

"Gee, Jessica," said Annie, "what about the soccer game next week?"

"You guys will have to do it without me," Jessica replied. "In fact," she added, her voice serious, "you really ought to get used to doing cheers without me. After this play is over, I expect I'll be on my way to New York."

"If you see my mother there, give her my regards," said Annie dryly. "But seriously, Jess, aren't you getting carried away? Do you really think this play will lead to an acting career?"

"Of course it will!" Paula said earnestly before Jessica could reply. Jessica stared at Paula for a few seconds before turning back to Annie and Elizabeth.

"It's only reasonable to assume that it will," Jessica said. "David Goodman is a famous director. Why would he bother with high school kids if he wasn't looking for new talent? And who's got more of it than me?"

"Jessica, you're too much!" said Robin, shaking her head. "I know reality isn't your strong point, but it would be nice if you'd come down to earth occasionally and show a little consideration to the rest of us on the cheerleading squad."

"Critics! Already I have critics!" said Jessica, dismissing them with a wave of her hand. "And opening night is still more than two weeks away. Well, I'd love to stay and chat, but it's time for me to exit stage left. My number-one fan awaits me. Liz, tell Mom and Dad I've gone to Sam's."

Elizabeth watched her twin stroll across the patio and disappear into the house. Annie and Robin were right. Jessica *was* getting carried away.

"You've got it all wrong!" Lila complained to Tracy Gilbert, pointing to the drawing on Tracy's clipboard. It was Tuesday afternoon and the girls were backstage in the school auditorium. "A real witch would never wear something like that! Back me up here, Jessica!"

Jessica and Paula stood nearby, watching Lila being measured for her costume. "Oh, I don't know, Lila," Jessica said sweetly. "It looks pretty witchy to me. And Annie and Rosa seem happy with the design."

"Traitor!"

"Lila, if you don't hold still, I'm never going to finish measuring you," Tracy said through the straight pins she held clutched between her teeth.

"But it's *gray*, for crying out loud!" Lila objected. "What kind of a costume designer are you? I think we should go with something more magical. Lavender, maybe, with glitter."

"Lila, you're a witch, not the Sugerplum Fairy." Tracy sounded as though she was losing patience.

"And witches should be sultry and alluring.

61

That baggy thing doesn't even have a waistline! Young, beautiful, sexy witches would sell a lot more tickets."

"It's rough being a witch with fashion sense," sighed Jessica.

"You don't have to *smirk*!" Lila complained. "A lot you care, anyhow. I've seen the drawings for *your* outfits."

"They're great, aren't they?" Paula said with a dreamy sigh.

"Tracy," Jessica said, "are you still planning to do my first fitting on Thursday?"

"That's right. But we'll be in the home ec room instead of here," Tracy answered, taking the pins from her mouth. "Your costumes are pretty complicated, so you can expect to be there most of the rehearsal period. Mr. Goodman says it's OK; he won't be going over any of your scenes that afternoon."

"Great!" said Jessica. "Oh, there's Mr. Goodman now. Come on, Paula, let's talk to him about you."

A few minutes later, Jessica and Paula stood with the director and his cute blond assistant, Frank O'Donnell. "Mr. Goodman, this is my friend Paula Perrine. She's been a big help the last week, working on my lines with me."

"Ah yes, we've met," said Mr. Goodman. He nodded at Paula. "Good afternoon, Ms. Perrine," he said. "And congratulations. If it's your help that has made Ms. Wakefield as well-prepared as she has been, you deserve my thanks."

Jessica felt confused and a little miffed. When had shy little Paula met the famous theatre director? Paula hadn't said anything about it to her. And where did he get off, congratulating Paula on Jessica's hard work? Oh well. At least he'd noticed it.

"Mr. Goodman," Jessica said graciously, "Paula wants to try out for the part of the gentlewoman."

"Excellent!" he said. "Mr. O'Donnell can hear her audition in the back of the auditorium while we rehearse the last half of act one, beginning with scene four."

A few minutes later, Jessica stood alone in the wings, awaiting her cue and watching the scene before hers.

"What's Paula doing with Frank?" whispered Lila, coming up behind Jessica. "They're having way too much fun for an audition!"

Jessica looked toward the back of the auditorium. Sure enough, Paula was standing very close to the good-looking assistant director. They didn't seem to be rehearsing. In fact, Paula was gabbing away as though she had known him all her life. And Frank couldn't take his eyes off her, Jessica noticed.

"I guess I'm a better role model than I thought," Jessica whispered back. "I told her she needed to come out of her shell. But I didn't think she'd . . ." Jessica frowned. "At least you've got to respect her taste in guys!"

In spite of her light tone, Jessica felt ambivalent

about Paula's quick turnaround. Just the week before, Paula had been so shy that she could barely start a conversation with a stranger, let alone a cute college boy. Now she was flirting with Frank as if she had had as much experience at it as Jessica herself. A person couldn't get over such shyness that quickly—could she?

No, of course not, Jessica told herself. Inside, Paula must be absolutely terrified, but Jessica had given her the courage to try to conquer her timidity. It was silly of Jessica to feel uncomfortable about her friend's successful efforts to be more sociable. She should just be happy for Paula.

"Only look up clear," Jessica said. She was finishing up the last speech of her scene and remembering Elizabeth's explanation of what the lines really meant. "To alter favor ever is to fear."

Bill, looking frightened but determined as Macbeth, nodded in agreement. Then he exited, leaving her alone onstage. Jessica looked offstage in the direction Bill had gone and prepared to say her last line.

Then she froze. Paula had apparently finished auditioning for Frank because Jessica saw them both standing in the wings, laughing with a group of cast members. The group included Lila, Annie, and Winston, but Paula was obviously the center of attention. She was saying something that everyone seemed to find terribly funny.

Paula caught Jessica's eye and stopped laughing abruptly.

That two-faced traitor was laughing at me, Jessica realized. Suddenly, she was enraged.

Jessica collected her wits and slowly pronounced her last line: "Leave all the rest to me."

"Excellent work, Jessica!" called Mr. Goodman. Jessica turned to the center of the auditorium, where the white-haired director sat.

"I particularly like what you've done with the last line of the scene," he raved. "The dark intensity you brought to it was quite effective, coming after that pregnant pause." He raised his voice. "I want it a little quieter backstage while we're rehearsing! Mr. O'Donnell, please remove the source of the distraction."

Jessica walked offstage slowly, fists clenched. When she reached the area where Paula and the others had been talking, they were gone.

When Elizabeth slipped through the stage door a few minutes later, she could hear her twin's voice from the stage as Jessica and Bill rehearsed their next scene.

"Hello, Frank," Elizabeth said, walking up behind the assistant director. "You're just the man I'm looking for."

"Well, you've found me," he joked. He turned, and Elizabeth saw that Paula was standing very close to him, with her hand on his arm. *What a transformation!* she thought. Jessica had said she was helping Paula be more outgoing, but Elizabeth was amazed to see that she had become so friendly with the assistant director so quickly.

She had to admit that Paula looked radiantly happy.

"Hi, Paula," Elizabeth said. Then she turned back to Frank. "I need to get the full crew list from you for the play programs." He nodded and began rummaging in the portfolio he carried.

"Elizabeth, you'll never believe it!" Paula said. "Frank is letting me play the role of the gentlewoman!" She laughed nervously. "Now all I have to do is get up the nerve to go onstage."

"Don't believe her," Frank teased, looking up from his papers. "You should have heard her audition. She's a natural."

"Congratulations, Paula," Elizabeth said sincerely. "I knew you could do it."

"I *hope* I can do it," Paula said quietly. Suddenly she looked very serious. She walked closer to the curtain and stared out past the stage at the rows of seats in the darkened auditorium.

Elizabeth knew that Jessica and Bill were on the other side of the curtain, but their scene called for them to stay on the far end of the stage, out of sight from this angle. She could hear their voices as they ran through their lines. Applause burst out from the cast and crew sitting in the audience.

"Look out there," Paula said in a hushed tone, still gazing out past the curtain. "There's nothing else like the theatre. Can you imagine any greater thrill? You can lose yourself in a character. And if you're good—I mean *really* good—you can play any part, no matter how unbelievable, and people will hang on every word."

She turned to Elizabeth and Frank. "And the

applause," she whispered earnestly. "There's nothing like the applause. It's like being loved by hundreds of people you don't even know."

Paula turned back to stare out at the auditorium, and Elizabeth felt tears welling up in her own eyes. Suddenly, she understood Paula's fascination with this play. To a girl with an unhappy family life, the outpouring of love from the audience must seem like heaven. She was glad that Paula had earned a role in the play. Paula deserved that happiness more than anyone Elizabeth knew.

"I got it!" said Paula, catching up with Jessica in the school parking lot after rehearsal. "I got the part of the gentlewoman! I always thought I would be too scared even to try out! And I owe it all to you, Jessica."

"Congratulations, Paula," Jessica said stiffly. "Maybe you're not as shy as we thought."

She couldn't get out of her mind the image of "shy" little Paula flirting with tall, confident Frank. And what about that incident backstage, while Jessica was finishing up her scene? For the last week, Paula had been acting as though she adored Jessica. But Jessica was *positive* that Paula and the others backstage had been laughing at her.

Don't be silly, Jessica chastised herself. *They could have been talking about anything.*

But if Paula hadn't been ridiculing her, then why had she stopped talking and laughing when she saw that Jessica was watching?

"Jessica," Paula said quietly, "is something wrong? You look upset."

Jessica opened her mouth to confront her, and then closed it. Anything she said would sound idiotic. She couldn't exactly order Paula not to talk to other people and not to tell jokes!

I'm being ridiculous, she told herself. Paula was making new friends. What was so suspicious about that?

Jessica tried to smile. "No, nothing's wrong," she lied. "I was just thinking about, uh, the blocking for my sleepwalking scene," Jessica said quickly. "I want to make it very powerful and eerie, but I haven't decided exactly how to do it."

"I'm sure the blocking will be incredible if *you* design it," said Paula, her eyes glowing. "Let me know if I can help—not that I'd be able to add anything to your creative ideas."

"Stop it!" Jessica yelled, losing control. "Stop telling me every three seconds how wonderful I am! And stop telling me how pathetic you are. I'm getting sick of it!"

Paula looked stunned. Both girls was silent for a moment, and Jessica watched a tear roll slowly down Paula's face.

"You *are* upset," Paula said slowly. "I'm sorry, Jessica."

"And stop apologizing all the time!"

"You're absolutely right, Jessica," Paula said tearfully. She lowered her voice, and Jessica could hardly hear her. "You keep telling me I should have confidence in myself," she sobbed. "*I try so hard*—and sometimes I think I'm making progress. But then I hear my father's voice inside my head *telling me I'll never be good at anything.*"

Jessica was aghast. "I'm the one who should be sorry," she cried. "I can't believe I said something so awful to you when you've been so nice to me. Can you ever forgive me for being such a jerk?"

"Of course I forgive you, Jessica," said Paula, smiling through her tears. "You're the best friend I ever had." She reached out to Jessica and hugged her.

When the girls separated, Jessica found that she was crying, too. She wiped her eyes with the back of her hand. "I don't know what got into me," she began. "I guess I'm just so uptight about the play—"

"There's no need to explain," said Paula understandingly, "as long as we're still friends."

"Of course we are!" Jessica said fervently. "Are we still on for practicing our lines at lunch tomorrow?"

"You bet!" said Paula. She waved and began to walk off in the direction of the bus stop.

Jessica climbed slowly into the twins' Jeep. She was about to shut the door when she remembered something.

"Paula!" she called hesitantly. "I forgot to ask you . . ."

Paula walked back toward the Jeep. "What is it?" she asked.

"Oh, it's no big deal," said Jessica. "I'm just a little confused, as usual." She smiled and shrugged self-effacingly. "I was thinking about what Mr. Goodman said when I introduced you two. You never told me that you'd met him before."

Paula flushed slightly. "Oh, but I hadn't . . . well, not really. I dropped my books the other day, right outside the auditorium." She laughed. "I'm the world's biggest klutz, Jessica. I'd give anything to be graceful like you. Anyhow, Mr. Goodman was coming out of the auditorium at the time, so he stopped and helped me pick my books up."

"Oh, I see," said Jessica, relaxing. "I figured it was something like that."

I've got to be more understanding, Jessica resolved as she drove home. The poor kid had been through some awful experiences; it was no wonder that she was a little peculiar at times. Her suspicions about Paula were obviously unfounded,

Six

"Hi, Annie," Paula said, joining her in the cafeteria line Wednesday. "Have you finished that awful English assignment? I was up half the night working on it!"

"I've still got to get though the last page of questions," Annie admitted. "I was planning on finishing them in study hall. Walt Whitman is about the most boring poet who ever lived."

"That's for sure," said Paula. "And if Mr. Collins weren't so good-looking, I think I'd want to strangle him for asking such hard questions! But now that I've gotten through them all, I may be able to give you a hand."

"Paula, you're a lifesaver," Annie said gratefully. "I can use all the help I can get."

"So where are Lila and Amy today?"

"They're waiting at our usual table," said

Annie. "They both brought lunch from home." She grimaced. "And from the looks of those hamburgers, I wish I had, too."

"I've never seen purplish hamburgers before," Paula said, putting two of them on her tray. "I don't know if I should eat them or turn them in as a chemistry experiment."

"You must be starving," Annie said. "One of those gross things is about all I could possibly eat."

"Oh, they're not both for me," Paula said, laughing. "Jessica and I are rehearsing together in a few minutes. She asked me to pick up some lunch for her, too." She reached forward to take two brownies from the counter. "I know what you're thinking, Annie, but there's no need to worry. Jessica's not taking advantage of me. I don't mind doing her a favor now and then."

"I'm sorry, Paula. It's none of my business, but I can't help being a little worried about you. You're always so eager to be helpful. Sometimes a friendship can get kind of one-sided without a person even realizing it."

"My friendship with Jessica may look one-sided, but it's really not," Paula assured her. "I get more out of it than anyone realizes."

"That may be so, but you're so different when Jessica's around. You clam up as soon as she walks into the room."

Paula laughed. "Maybe it's because Jessica is so confident and lively. I just love sitting back and listening to her talk! I guess I'm hoping some of it will rub off on me."

72

"Well, one Jessica Wakefield is plenty for any school!" Annie said, laughing. "Especially with the way she's been acting lately. So don't go changing too much to be like her. I like you just fine—exactly the way you are."

Paula smiled. "Thanks, Annie," she said. "You don't know how much that means to me."

The girls made their way through the crowded lunchroom to the table where Lila and Amy were waiting.

"That's a marvelous handbag, Lila!" Paula exclaimed. "You have such exquisite taste. Is it new?"

"Of course it's new," said Lila, smiling proudly. "Why don't you sit down and join us, Paula?"

"Thanks, but I can stay only a minute. I'm meeting Jessica in the drama room."

"Are you helping her write her acceptance speech for the Tony award?" Lila asked. Her tone was acid, but Paula laughed.

"How is Her Highness?" asked Amy. "I hardly see her at all anymore. I guess she's much too busy to remember any of us little people who knew her before she was such a big star."

"I'm sure Jessica doesn't mean to neglect her friends," Paula said loyally. "She's just a little preoccupied right now with this production."

When it came to Jessica, Paula's loyalty was definitely misplaced, thought Annie. "So what's everyone doing this weekend?" Annie asked, changing the subject. "Is anything exciting going on?"

"Actually, I was hoping to get a group of peo-

73

ple together at Secca Lake," said Paula. "I've never been there, but I hear it's a great place for a cookout. I'll do all the planning and bring all the food. All you have to do is show up with your bathing suits!"

"What a great idea!" said Amy. "But you don't have to do everything yourself. Let us help with the food."

"Absolutely not," said Paula. "It's my way of thanking all of you for making me feel so welcome in Sweet Valley. Who else should I invite? Amy, you'll bring Barry, won't you?" She counted on her fingers. "Then there's Winston and Maria, Bill and DeeDee—"

"Of course you'll be asking Jessica, Elizabeth, Sam, and Todd," said Annie.

"Well, I'll invite them," Paula replied, "but I don't think they'll come. Jessica's already asked me to rehearse with her Saturday morning, and I know she'll want to spend the afternoon rehearsing by herself. Her dedication is so inspirational."

Lila rolled her eyes.

"And of course, Elizabeth has her hands full with the publicity work," Paula concluded.

"Elizabeth told me this morning that you've been a big help on the publicity, Paula," Annie said. "I didn't know you were working on that, too."

"Oh, it's nothing," Paula said. "I just made a couple of phone calls for her one day." She paused and looked at them intently. "But please," she implored, "don't anyone tell Jessica!"

"Why not?" Lila asked.

Paula's voice grew quiet. "I guess it's kind of silly," she said. "I just don't want Jessica to get the idea that anything about this play is more important to me than helping her with her role."

"Well, your secret's safe with us," said Lila. "Outside of rehearsals, we hardly ever see Jessica anymore. Even spending a Saturday afternoon at Secca Lake with us would be much too *ordinary* for an actress of Ms. Wakefield's caliber."

"Well, call me ordinary, but *I'm* looking forward to an afternoon at the lake," said Annie.

"*Where have you been, Paula?*" came Jessica's voice. Annie turned to see Jessica striding up to the table. "You were supposed to be in the drama room with me *ten minutes ago!*"

"Lighten up, Jessica," said Amy. "It's not that big a deal."

"Mind your own business!" Jessica demanded. She whirled to face Paula again. "You said you'd bring my lunch and my script—and that you'd be there at twelve-ten. It's twelve-twenty! I'm not going to have time to work out that scene for rehearsal today, thanks to you!"

"Jessica Wakefield," yelled Lila, "What's gotten into you!"

"It's all right," Paula said, laughing weakly. "I don't mind, really. I'm used to being ordered around."

Annie thought about Paula's father. How could Jessica be so cruel to the girl?

At least Jessica had the grace to blush. "I'm sorry, Paula," she stammered. "I didn't mean—" She turned and fled.

75

"Are you OK, Paula?" asked Annie. "I can't believe she would treat you like that!"

"Don't worry about it," said Paula, smiling. "Jessica's just working too hard and feeling nervous about the play." She laughed. "Jessica talks like that at least once a day and then apologizes. She doesn't mean anything by it, so I don't take it personally."

"Now I'm *really* glad she'll be too busy to come to Secca Lake Saturday," said Amy. "I'd much rather spend the afternoon with you, Paula."

"I'm surprised to see you here, Jessica," Paula said, running into her outside the auditorium door Thursday after school. "I thought you had a costume fitting in the home ec room."

"I do," Jessica said coldly. She knew she was being unreasonable, but she felt annoyed. Her schedule was none of Paula's business. "But I left my history book backstage during study hall today."

She reached for the door, but Paula moved in front of it.

"Don't go in there, Jessica!" Paula said quickly. "I mean, there's no need for you to be late to your costume fitting. You know how the production crew is. If you set foot in there, they'll have you onstage to test the lighting effects or go over some dialogue, and you'll never make it to the fitting."

There was some truth to that, Jessica admitted to herself. But why was Paula so insistent?

"I'm coming over to your house to rehearse

tonight," Paula continued. "I'll find your history book and bring it with me." Paula smiled sweetly. "You'd better go to your costume fitting. And don't worry about your history book. Leave it all to me."

"Thanks for the milkshake, Sam," said Jessica, sinking back into the passenger seat of his car that night. "I needed to get out of the house for a few minutes. It was nice of you to drive all that way to take me out."

"I thought that a strawberry shake from Casey's would be a sure cure for your problems, Jess. Unfortunately, it doesn't seem to have helped much. You still look pretty out of it."

"I am," she replied. "I'm convinced that Steven was right about *Macbeth* being cursed. I've got this awful feeling that something is going to go terribly wrong with this production."

"There's no such thing as a curse, Jess. You've got an industrial-strength case of stage fright. That's all."

"No, Sam. It's more than that. And I still can't get Paula out of my mind. I don't know what it is about her that makes me so crazy. I can't believe I blew up at her in the cafeteria yesterday for no reason."

"It does sound as though you flipped out," Sam agreed. "Paula must be quite a girl to be so calm and understanding when you lay into her like that."

"She *is* understanding," Jessica said. "I should be glad to have her as a friend."

"Then why aren't you?"

"I don't know," Jessica said, rubbing her hands together nervously. "I just don't know."

"You said that she was at your house rehearsing tonight. You didn't have any problems, did you?"

"No, we didn't," Jessica said. "She seemed as anxious to please as ever. And I wasn't the least bit mean to her this time. But still, I felt kind of uneasy—like she's hiding something from me."

"Jessica, you're being paranoid again."

"Lila said at rehearsal today that Paula played tennis last weekend with her and Amy and Annie. Doesn't that seem weird to you? *I* usually play tennis with Lila, Amy, and Annie. But nobody asked *me* to play last weekend. And why didn't Paula tell me about it herself?"

"Listen to yourself, Jessica! You sound like you're jealous of Paula because she has *friends*. I'm sure she wasn't trying to hide it from you. It probably just never came up in conversation. You don't tell her everything you do."

"That's true," Jessica agreed. "It's just that Paula seems to have friends lately, and I don't."

"Now that's the most ridiculous thing I've ever heard you say! You've got more friends than anybody in Sweet Valley."

"I used to," said Jessica, troubled. "But they've changed. Everyone acts like they'd rather not have me around at all."

"That's crazy," Sam said impatiently. "You're just so busy with the play that you don't have much time for them. Maybe Lila and Amy are feeling a little neglected."

"I guess so. I've got to stop overreacting. And I've got to stop imagining crazy things about Paula. Paula's my friend, and she's had a terrible life. I should be as understanding with her as she is with me."

"Now you're talking," said Sam.

Jessica was silent for the rest of the ride home. When he stopped the car in front of the Wakefields' house, she leaned over and kissed him on the cheek.

"Bye," she whispered. Then she jumped out of the car and ran up the dark lawn to the house.

"Where's Jessica today?" asked Maria at noon on Friday. She spread her arms to indicate the high school's sunny courtyard. "This is her favorite place to eat lunch."

"The queen is rehearsing, as usual," said Lila, "with Paula, her loyal subject."

"That's the same excuse Jessica gave me for backing out of our plans for last night," said Amy. "I guess it shouldn't surprise me anymore." With her finger, she tilted her nose upward. "After all, she is a star, you know."

"In my opinion, Jessica is taking this stardom thing much too far," commented Lila.

"She *is* getting to be annoying at rehearsals," said Annie, unwrapping a sandwich. "Did you hear the way she yelled at Emily at practice Wednesday? All Emily did was miss a cue. I don't see what the big deal was."

"I didn't know Emily was in the play," said Amy. "I wouldn't have thought that Shakespeare was her thing." Petite Emily Mayer, a junior, was the drummer for Sweet Valley High's most popular rock band, the Droids.

"Well, it's a very small part," said Lila. "Emily's got to be there anyhow since she's doing the drumbeats and the knocking sounds that the script calls for, so she decided to try out for a part as well. She's Lady Macduff—you know, she comes onstage, her son is murdered in front of her, and then the killers chase her offstage. It's just one scene." Lila leaned back and adjusted the straps on her tank top to take full advantage of the midday sun. "Besides," she continued, "Emily's not the only unlikely Shakespeare buff around. Jessica Wakefield wasn't exactly a Shakespeare fanatic herself before now."

"This play is just full of surprises," said Amy. "I couldn't believe Jennifer got mononucleosis and had to drop out as Jessica's understudy. But I was even more surprised to hear that Paula is taking her place."

"It is pretty amazing," agreed Lila. "I mean, Paula's very nice—though I'll never understand her fascination with Jessica—but she's so shy."

"I guess Jessica must be pleased." said Maria. "She *says* she likes Paula—though it looks like a bizarre friendship, if you ask me."

"I, for one, am glad for Paula," said Annie. "She's always so generous and cheerful."

"She certainly deserves *something* for putting up with Jessica's prima donna act!" said Lila.

"Of course, Paula will never actually get to play Lady Macbeth," Amy pointed out. "Wild horses couldn't keep Jessica away from the performances!"

"True," Lila commented. "But it's a nice little boost for Paula's ego."

"Speaking of Paula, have any of you taken a good look at her lately?" Amy asked. "Whatever Jessica's doing with her sure is working. Her hair looks a lot better since she started wearing it loose."

"And she's dressing with a little more flair," said Lila. "But she really needs to empty her closet and buy a whole new wardrobe." She wrinkled her nose. "Maybe Tracy can design something for her."

"Don't be so hard on Tracy," said Annie. "Rosa and I *like* our witches' costumes. Witches are *supposed* to be dark and ugly."

"Then it's a good thing I'm a fantastic actress, because dark and ugly is going to take quite a bit of acting for *me!*"

"Thanks for the lift, Annie," said Jessica on Tuesday evening. "Elizabeth took the Jeep downtown to deliver her article about the play to the *Sweet Valley News*, and Lila left rehearsal early to play tennis with Amy. I'd have been stranded without you."

"Oh, it's no problem," said Annie as they left the high school parking lot in her silver Ford Escort. "Besides, I love driving down your street," she added wistfully. "Mom and I have been in that little apartment only since the divorce, but it seems like forever. It's nice to remind myself of what a real neighborhood looks like." She paused for a moment. "But where was Paula today? I know she would have been happy to give you a ride—even to the moon, if you asked her to."

"Paula doesn't have a car," said Jessica. "She only borrows one sometimes from the people she lives with. This afternoon she said she had to take the bus downtown to run a lot of errands. She didn't even have time to rehearse with me tonight."

"You know, Jess, I've really gotten to like Paula. She seemed so shy at first, but she's got a terrific sense of humor. It's great that she was picked to replace Jennifer as your understudy. I know how much it means to her."

Jessica froze. "She was picked for what?"

"You know, to understudy Lady Macbeth." Annie stopped the car at a stop sign and turned to look at Jessica. "You mean you didn't know?"

Jessica was stunned. "When did this happen?"

"Thursday," said Annie as they turned onto Jessica's street. "Oh, that explains it. Weren't you in a costume fitting?"

"But we rehearsed together all weekend. Paula never even mentioned it."

Annie pulled to a stop in front of the Wakefields' house. "I guess she assumed you already knew."

Seven

"Wait up, Paula!" called Jessica in the school hall-way the next morning. "I want to talk to you!"

"Sorry, Jessica, but I really have to go. I'll be late for homeroom."

"Then you'll have to be late," Jessica said shortly.

"Oh no!" said Paula, her eyes wide. "You're mad at me, Jessica. What's the matter? Have I done something wrong?"

Jessica stopped short. Was she being too harsh? Paula looked terrified—Jessica's opinion seemed to matter so much to her. But then why hadn't she told Jessica about becoming her understudy? It didn't make sense.

Jessica looked the sophomore in the eye and took a deep breath. "Paula," she began in a steady voice, "I heard last night that you're my new understudy in the play—and that Mr. Good-man announced it almost a week ago. Why didn't you tell me?''

"I'm so sorry, Jessica," Paula said ardently. "I guess it sounds silly, but I didn't think it was important. You're too much of a professional ever to miss a performance."

"But Paula, you never even told me you were trying out. Why did you go behind my back? I thought you were my friend!"

"Oh, I am your friend, Jessica. That's why I did it. I just had to try out. It was you who gave me the confidence. You made me see that I could be somebody." She paused, and Jessica was afraid she was about to cry. Instead, she continued in a quiet voice, "Even my own family never did that for me."

Poor kid, thought Jessica. *She finally has a friend —me—and I'm insensitive enough to doubt her.*

"I'm sorry, Paula," she said. "Maybe I jumped to conclusions."

The younger girl smiled and looked relieved. Then the bell rang and Paula ran off toward her homeroom class. But Jessica stood, watching her.

This is a dream come true for Paula, she thought. *And I'm supposed to be her friend. So why can't I be happy for her?*

"I have to talk to you," Jessica said to her twin that evening, walking into the Wakefields' kitchen.

"Good," said Elizabeth, pouring rice into a measuring cup. "You can talk while you help me make dinner—seeing as how it's your turn to do it anyway."

"OK, Liz. I'll make the salad." She picked up the head of lettuce that Elizabeth had placed on the counter and started rinsing it in the sink. "I'm not even sure if I should tell you," Jessica said. "You'll say I'm being too suspicious. But I really think there's something weird going on, and I don't know who else to talk to."

Elizabeth was used to her twin's mood swings, but it wasn't like Jessica to look this genuinely miserable. "Hold on! You're making even less sense than usual. Why don't you start at the beginning?"

"It's Paula. I know what a rough life she's had, Liz. And I know how much she's helped me. But she's hiding something from me, and I don't know why."

"You can't be serious. Paula is the sweetest, most open, most generous girl we know. And she thinks the world of you."

"I was afraid you wouldn't believe me. But Liz, Mr. Goodman made her my understudy almost a week ago, and she never even told me about it! Why would she keep that a secret?"

"I don't know, Jessica. She respects you so much. Maybe she was embarrassed. You know how shy she is."

"How shy she *pretends to be*, you mean. I know I've been encouraging her to be more outgoing, but I can't believe she could change that much so quickly—and only when she doesn't think I'm watching. You should see the way she flirts with Frank O'Donnell in rehearsal every day."

"Oh, I get it," said Elizabeth, putting her hands on her hips. "You're jealous because a cute college boy is paying attention to Paula instead of you."

"It's not that. She told me she would never have the guts to wear her hair and makeup the way I taught her, but then she started showing up at school all decked out like a fashion model —well, maybe not quite *that* decked out, but she sure looks a lot more stylish. So why does she still dress like a geek when she comes over here to rehearse with just me?"

"Maybe it's because you're the only person she feels she can be herself with, Jessica. You're supposed to be her friend. You should be happy that she's becoming more popular."

"Liz, at a rehearsal last week I saw her backstage, laughing with a big group of people. She stopped cold as soon as she saw me. I'm sure she was laughing at me."

"It isn't like you to be this suspicious!"

Jessica sighed. "You don't understand."

"What is there to understand? After everything that poor girl has been through, you're the one who should try to be a little more understanding."

"I guess you're right," Jessica conceded. "I'm just so confused."

Confused is right, Elizabeth thought. *But Jessica's been working awfully hard since rehearsals started. The stress must be getting to her. Maybe it would help to get her mind off Paula.*

"You know, Jess, you've been so busy with rehearsals that you haven't even asked about the poster contest," she said, changing the subject. "David Prentiss's design centers around you as Lady Macbeth in the sleepwalking scene."

"I saw his rough sketches," Jessica said. "He really is good, isn't he?"

"He's fabulous, but he's got some tough competition. DeeDee's idea, with Bill as Macbeth, turned out beautifully. In fact, we've got at least a dozen entries! But you can see them for yourself. A lot of people hung their designs up in the art room today for everyone to look at."

"Oh, I didn't know," Jessica said, preoccupied.

That's odd, Elizabeth thought as she lowered the heat under the rice. The poster design had seemed so important to her twin a few days earlier. Jessica must have spent the whole day in a daze because of her fears about Paula. *Oh well*, Elizabeth reflected, *this isn't the first time Jessica's let her imagination run away with her.*

"I bet Olivia's working on something terrific for the contest," Elizabeth continued. "She says she won't show it to anyone, except the judges, until after the winner is announced on Friday. I can't wait to see it!"

"Liz, you know how important it is to me to have my picture on the posters, don't you?" Jessica wheedled. "After all, I've been working so hard on this play!"

Now *that* sounded more like the Jessica Wakefield her sister knew.

"Don't even think about it, Jessica. The contest

will be totally impartial. Besides, Mr. Goodman and his staff are doing the judging, not me."

"But he'd listen to you, Liz. He can't stop telling everyone how wonderful you are. Maybe you could just give him a little push toward a design that features your own beloved twin sister."

"No way, Jess," said Elizabeth. "But cheer up. David's poster is fantastic. He could win it without any help from me!"

DeeDee's set designs look great, Jessica said to herself during rehearsal Thursday afternoon. She watched from the wings as the witches made their entrance for act one, scene three.

"Look what I have," boasted Lila onstage, as the first witch. *So Lila's finally memorized her lines*, thought Jessica. Her friend's witch voice was a perfect imitation of the one in *The Wizard of Oz*.

"Show me, show me," Annie recited with a cackle.

"Here I have a pilot's thumb," answered Lila, "wracked as homeward he did come.... You know, this is really gross!"

Jessica covered her mouth to keep from laughing out loud.

"Ms. Fowler!" called Mr. Goodman. "Please recite the words as Shakespeare wrote them, with no editorial comments."

"But the words are so disgusting!"

"Come on, Lila," Annie urged. "They're no worse than the ones Rosa and I have to say."

"Oh, all right," said Lila. They began the scene again.

A few minutes later, Jessica watched as Bill and Winston made their entrance.

"What are these," asked Winston as Banquo, pointing at Lila, Annie, and Rosa, "so withered, and so wild in their attire, that look not like the inhabitants of the earth, yet are on it?" As he spoke he looked directly at Lila.

Jessica saw Lila's eyes narrow. She knew just what her friend was thinking. If Lila could, she would probably choose this moment to turn Winston into a newt.

"You seem to understand me," continued Winston, motioning toward all three witches, "by each at once her choppy finger laying upon her skinny lips." He pointed directly at Lila. "You should be women, and yet your beards forbid me to interpret that you are so."

"That's it!" cried Lila, stamping her foot. "I will not stand for these insults!"

"Lila, it's all part of the play," said Rosa, sighing.

"I don't care!" said Lila. "I refuse to be humiliated!"

"Ms. Fowler," said Mr. Goodman, running his hand through his white hair. "You must stick to the script!"

"Lila," Winston began, "I was looking at you when I said that only because you're doing such a terrific job playing this difficult role. Even without the costume, you're totally believable as a witch. It's uncanny!"

"Hmph," said Lila.

"I give up," said Mr. Goodman. "Lights!" The

stage brightened. "Witches, take a break. Lady Macbeth, Doctor, and Gentlewoman, prepare to go over act five, scene one—the sleepwalking scene. Do we have sets?"

"Not yet, Mr. Goodman," said DeeDee, emerging from backstage. A stripe of yellow paint blazed across her forehead. "It'll be Monday before the castle interiors are finished."

"Then we'll do the scene with what's onstage now—but with the proper lighting," Mr. Goodman said impatiently. "Start with Lady Macbeth's entrance. Places, everyone."

Paula materialized and brushed by Jessica to take her place. Jessica hadn't even known she was at rehearsal. Adam Tyner, a senior Jessica barely knew, was already onstage.

Mr. Goodman clapped his hands, trying to be heard over the buzz of students working throughout the auditorium. "Enter, Lady Macbeth," he called.

Jessica stepped into a pale circle of light, and the room went silent. In her left hand was a tall candlestick, unlit for now. She moved slowly across the darkened stage, and the circle of bluish light moved with her. As she walked she turned her head from side to side as if searching for something that wasn't there.

The mood in the room had changed almost instantly from pandemonium to a kind of rapt quiet, and Jessica realized with a tingle that it was her acting that had caused the transformation. She *was* Lady Macbeth, consumed by guilt and slowly losing her mind.

"Here she comes," said Paula, playing the gentlewoman. "This is her very guise, and, upon my life, fast asleep! Observe her; stand close."

"How came she by that light?" asked Adam, as the doctor. He and Paula were standing on one side of the stage. Yellowish-white spotlights bathed them in a normal, daytime sort of light, in contrast to the pale glow that surrounded Jessica.

The two commented on her actions as Jessica set down the candle and began rubbing her hands together fitfully.

"It is an accustomed action with her, to seem thus washing her hands," said Paula. "I have known her continue in this a quarter of an hour."

As she spoke Paula walked forward, and her shadow fell across Jessica's face. *This wasn't the way we rehearsed it yesterday*, Jessica thought angrily. *Why is that little twerp trying to upstage me?* Jessica stepped forward into the light.

"Yet here's a spot," she said sadly, gazing at her hand.

"Excellent, Jessica!" said Mr. Goodman, cutting her off. Jessica was thrilled. The director never used a student's first name unless he was really impressed. "I appreciate the effort you've put into blocking out this scene," he continued. "But we're trying something slightly different now."

Jessica stared. She had worked so hard on the movements for her sleepwalking.

"But Mr. Goodman, yesterday you said you liked the way I did it."

"Yes, but I want you to do it another way today. As the gentlewoman speaks she will walk forward, as she did that time. But you do not walk forward. You stay in place, and your face is in her shadow as you say your first line.''

''But Mr. Goodman,'' Jessica protested, ''this is one of the most powerful points in the play. The audience should be able to see me when I say that line.''

''I think you'll change your mind as soon as you try it this way,'' the director insisted. ''It lends an air of introspection and mystery. You will move forward a little later, before your next speech.''

He smiled at Jessica and gestured toward Paula. ''Your friend Ms. Perrine recommended the change; she has an excellent eye for stage direction.''

Jessica quietly performed the scene the way Mr. Goodman—and Paula—wanted it. But inside she was numb. *Paula* had changed her blocking. *Paula* had been talking with the director about Jessica's role in the play—*without Jessica*. Why was Paula deciding how Jessica should play her part?

By that time Adam had delivered his next line and Jessica had moved forward, ready to begin her speech. Although she was no longer standing in Paula's shadow, she felt as if she were.

Eight

"Jessica Wakefield," said Lila, shaking a french fry at her friend, "can't you forget about the play for one little lunch period?"

Jessica put down her script. "How can I forget about the play?" she asked. "We've got only a week before opening night! I've been taking notes in rehearsals this week, and I'm really getting worried. Did you know that Rosa screwed up *two lines in one scene* the other day? And Tony Alimenti may be gorgeous, but he can't tell his stage right from his stage left!"

"Playing a queen doesn't give you the right to tell everyone else how to play their parts," Lila pointed out.

"You *have* been a little bossy, Jessica," Annie said diplomatically.

"A little bossy? She's a real prima donna!" said Lila.

"Not to mention a pain in the neck!" said Amy.

"I think you're all being too hard on Jessica," Paula put in quietly. "Playing Lady Macbeth is a huge responsibility. And Jessica is such a talented actress. It's only natural for her to expect the same dedication from everyone else."

Jessica turned on Paula. "If I need your help, I'll ask for it!" she snapped, blue-green eyes flashing.

This is just too much, thought Lila. "You know, Jessica," she said, "a lot of people are getting sick and tired of the way you're treating everyone. Paula may be about the only fan you have left."

Jessica blushed, and Lila was glad to see that she at least had the grace to look mortified. Maybe Jessica really hadn't realized how badly she had been treating her friends.

"I'm sorry, Paula," she said. "I'm sorry, everyone. I'm just so tense."

"It's OK, Jessica," said Paula. "We understand."

"At least *one* of us does," said Lila.

"Well, I've got the perfect solution to all our problems," said Amy. "A cheeseburger for each of us, and a big order of onion rings, split five ways. Remember, we decided to go to the Dairi Burger this evening, after you theatrical types finish rehearsal. We haven't been out together in ages!"

"And you all can help me plan the cast party I'm hosting on opening night," said Lila.

"Great!" said Annie. "Also, the poster contest

winner will be announced at rehearsal today. Soon, they'll be hanging Jessica's picture all over town!"

"Some people in the cast would like to see *Jessica* hanging!" Lila said. "But seriously, Jessica's face may not even win the contest."

"Of course it will," said Paula, gazing at Jessica.

Jessica stared back at her wordlessly.

"DeeDee's poster with Bill on it has just as good a chance as David's design," said Amy.

"That's right," Lila agreed. "And everyone's expecting Olivia Davidson's to be great, too, though she's keeping it secret until the judging. Honestly, Jess, I don't know what good it does to have a sister in high places if she won't pull a few strings now and then."

"Well, no matter which poster wins, we're going to the Dairi Burger to celebrate!" Annie declared. "Are you coming, Jess?"

Jessica looked up at her, startled. "I can't," she said.

"Forget it, Jessica," Amy cut in. "You're not allowed to stay home and rehearse tonight. We're going to get your mind off this play if it kills you."

"Or kills us!" Lila said.

"No, I really can't," Jessica insisted. "My brother's coming over tonight. I thought I'd just stay home and watch television with him."

"It's hard to believe a guy as cute as Steven can't find a date on a Friday night," Annie said, sighing.

"He *could* find one if he wanted one," Jessica argued. "It's just that he'd rather sit home with me."

"What about Sam?" Lila asked. "Didn't you already tell Sam you'd be at the Dairi Burger tonight, Jess?"

"Well, yes," said Jessica. "But it won't make any difference if I don't show up. He said he's got to stay home and study." Jessica paused before going on. "Paula, why don't you go along with the others? It'll be nice for you."

"Oh, I can't," said Paula. "I've still got some lines to memorize for the understudy role—not that I'll ever really need them for a performance." She stopped and smiled worshipfully at Jessica.

Paula had hardly taken her eyes off Jessica for the past half-hour, Lila noticed. But rather than reveling in Paula's adoration, Jessica was pretending not to notice. In fact, she was looking around the group at everyone *but* Paula. *What a waste of perfectly good admiration*, thought Lila again.

"But I don't mind not performing," Paula concluded. "Just watching you gives me a goal to work toward, Jessica."

Jessica turned to stare at Paula. There was a challenge in Jessica's cold eyes, but Paula's gaze never faltered. After a few moments, it was Jessica who abruptly turned away.

"Oh, Steven, it was awful!" wailed Jessica that evening. "You must be right about *Macbeth* having a curse on it. Poor David worked so hard on that wonderful poster design, and then Olivia ended up winning the contest!"

"I don't know, Jess," he replied, accepting a can of soda from her. "Elizabeth showed me a snapshot of Olivia's entry tonight, and I thought it was very good."

Elizabeth had gone to the movies with Todd, and their parents were having dinner with a client of Mrs. Wakefield's interior design firm. That left Jessica and Steven home alone for the evening. The television was on, but Jessica was too annoyed about the poster contest to be able to keep her mind on the movie they were watching.

"You obviously don't know anything about marketing a play," she said. "A beautiful, blond, tragic queen on the poster would sell a lot more tickets than ugly, shriveled witches. Besides, Lady Macbeth is the star. The witches' roles are minor."

"That's not the way I remember the play," Steven objected, digging into a bowl of pretzels. "For one thing, I thought *Mr.* Macbeth was the star."

"Well, he's got the most lines," Jessica admitted. "But he's so weak and wishy-washy. It's his lovely, strong wife who provides the dramatic impetus—"

"Dramatic impetus?" Steven guffawed. "That doesn't sound like the Jessica I know. Did you swallow a theatre critic?"

"Very funny. But Lady Macbeth really *should* be on the posters. I'll never forgive Elizabeth."

"Don't blame Elizabeth," said Steven. "You

know very well that she didn't make the decision—the judges did."

"But she didn't even try to influence them! I'm her very own twin sister. She knew how important it was to me."

"Yes, she did," said Steven. "And you should be proud of her for staying objective."

"But Steven, I was humiliated. There I was in the auditorium, with everyone expecting to see my face on the winning entry—after all, my sister *is* in charge of publicity. And then they unveil the poster, and instead of me, it shows *Lila* front and center, with the other witches behind her!"

"Face it, Jess. Olivia's concept is a good one," said Steven. "The witches are central to the play. And Liz told me everyone was blown away by Olivia's design."

"Well, maybe a few people were. Of course, Lila was mortified! The last thing she expected was to have her own face plastered all over town—in witch makeup!"

"I would've liked to see the expression on her face when the poster was unveiled," Steven admitted, laughing. He took a drink of soda. "So, how is Lila? I haven't seen her around here in ages. Have you two actresses been too busy with rehearsals to get together much lately?"

"The play *is* taking up a lot of time," sighed Jessica. "Outside of rehearsals and classes, the only person I ever spend time with anymore—besides Sam—is Paula Perrine. I've hardly spoken to Lila or Amy in weeks. But lately, Steven, I get the feeling that they don't *want* to see me."

"I thought you seemed kind of down," said her brother. "But I can't believe that there's serious trouble between you and the other musketeers."

"It's true! They make snide remarks about me playing a queen, and they say I'm not fun anymore," Jessica complained. "And last weekend a bunch of people got together at Secca Lake—*and I wasn't even invited!* Paula said that she suggested they invite me, but that Lila and Amy said not to bother! They figured I'd be too busy practicing my lines."

"It sounds like a simple misunderstanding, Jess," said Steven, handing her the pretzels. "And I can see why they'd think that. You *have* been pretty focused."

"What I really need is some time with my friends, away from school—without any mention of *Macbeth*," Jessica decided. "I hadn't realized how lonely I was feeling." She jumped up, overturning the bowl of pretzels. "And I'm going to do something about it right now!"

Prince Albert appeared out of nowhere and greedily began eating pretzels off the carpet.

"Would you mind watching the rest of this movie by yourself?" Jessica said to her brother. "I'd like to go down to the Dairi Burger and say hi to Lila and the gang."

"Abandoned again," Steven said in a mock tragic tone. "You just want an excuse to leave so that *I* have to clean up the pretzel crumbs."

"Thanks a million, Steven," Jessica called as she sprinted toward the door.

* * *

Jessica pulled the Jeep into the parking lot of the Dairi Burger. This was going to be great! A couple of hours with Lila, Amy, and Annie would do wonders for her mood. She'd order a milkshake and some onion rings, talk about what was on sale at the mall, and learn all the latest gossip.

"Even a famous actress has to take a night off occasionally," she rationalized as she walked toward the door of the popular hangout.

The place was busy, even for a Friday night. Noise and light spilled out the windows and overflowed into the parking lot. Jessica was glad that Paula had decided to stay home. She would feel better if she didn't have to deal with her at all that night.

Maybe she *had* been imagining things, she told herself. Maybe Paula really was as innocent, shy, and devoted as she appeared to be. Then Jessica shook her head. She just didn't believe it.

"Don't think about it!" Jessica told herself aloud. Tonight, she vowed, she was just going to have fun. She wasn't going to think about Paula Perrine or about the play.

Jessica pushed open the door and walked into the Dairi Burger. Then she stopped, stunned. Across the room in a corner booth sat Paula— with Sam.

Paula looked anything but shy now. For one thing, she had finally taken all of Jessica's advice about her appearance. Her makeup looked fantastic. Her brown hair, shimmering with highlights, swung loose around her face. She was wearing a sexy, stylish dress—a bright green floral print that left her shoulders bare.

But what surprised Jessica the most was the way she was acting. As Jessica watched, Paula leaned forward across the table provocatively. She whispered something in Sam's ear and then laughed. Sam laughed, too. In fact, Sam looked like he was having a *great* time.

"Jessica!" called Lila's voice. "Over here!"

Jessica turned and saw Lila and Amy beckoning to her from a nearby booth. *Oh, why didn't I stay home with Steven?* she asked herself. But it was too late now. She forced herself to join her friends.

"I'm glad you decided to come," said Amy. "We've been having the most marvelous time!" She turned to her boyfriend. "Move over, Barry, so we can fit Jessica in."

Jessica reluctantly sat down next to Amy and tried to smile.

"And Jess, Paula decided to come, too," said Annie. "She was sitting with us until half an hour ago. She was telling us the funniest stories. Paula is just full of surprises. I had no idea how witty she is!"

"She's still here somewhere," said Amy, glancing around.

Jessica was grateful that the crowd of people obscured Paula and Sam from her friends' sight.

"You know, Jessica," said Lila, "I was pretty skeptical about Paula at first—I mean, that wardrobe! But she's turned out to be really OK. And you should see how good she looks tonight. You've done wonders for her. She's really changed."

"Oh, I haven't done a thing," said Jessica quietly, fighting a feeling of panic. "And I think she was always a lot more sociable than she let on."

Jessica felt like crying. Lila, Amy, and Annie had always been *her* friends. But now they seemed to care more about Paula than they did about Jessica. She was sick of hearing people talk about how great Paula was. How had Paula gotten everyone to believe it? How had she managed to steal Jessica's place with her friends? *And now she's stealing my boyfriend!* Jessica thought sadly. Suddenly it seemed to Jessica that Paula was in control of almost everything that mattered to her —Sam, the play, Jessica's friends, and Jessica herself.

"Here comes Paula now!" Amy exclaimed. "And Sam's with her!"

Sam had spotted Jessica and was walking toward the table. Paula was with him, but she was hanging back. *Pretending to be shy again*, thought Jessica. She wasn't sure exactly what was going on, but she knew that she couldn't blow her cool now, in front of everyone. She pressed her lips together. She wouldn't say a word. No matter what she suspected about Paula, nobody would believe her, anyway. She had no proof that Paula was trying to take over anything.

"Jessica!" said Sam, holding out his arms. Jessica stood up stiffly and allowed herself to be hugged.

"Thanks for talking me into coming tonight, Jessica," said Paula. "I never would have, if it hadn't been for you."

"Great," Jessica mumbled under her breath. "It's nice to see you both," she said formally. "But I've got to get home. Steven's waiting for me."

She turned and bolted from the restaurant.

"Jessica!"

She heard Sam's voice behind her as she ran across the parking lot.

"Jessica, what's wrong?" he asked, catching up to her and putting a hand on her shoulder.

"What are you doing here?" she demanded, wheeling to face him. "I thought you had to study tonight!"

"I did have to study. But I finished early and decided I'd drive down to see you. You *did* tell me you'd be here, didn't you?"

"Well, yes. But I didn't expect to get here and find you flirting with Paula behind my back!"

"Flirting? Is that what you think? We were only talking, Jessica. She's interested in dirt bike racing and had some questions for me. What's gotten into you?"

"Dirt bike racing? How did she know you were into dirt bike racing?"

"I don't know." Sam shrugged. "You probably mentioned it to her once."

"No, Sam. I never did. I'm *sure* I didn't."

"So what's the big deal? Lila or Amy probably said something about it. She was sitting with them when I came in. She could have heard it from anyone. It's not exactly a deep, dark secret. What does it matter where she heard it? I told you, we were only talking!"

Jessica hugged herself and stared into the darkness at the other end of the parking lot. "You never look at me that way when we're *only talking*."

"Jessica, I don't know what's wrong with you lately. You know you're the only girl I care about. But you seem to go off the deep end whenever Paula's involved. She's a perfectly nice girl, she's got a great sense of humor, and she has nothing but good things to say about you! It's not like you to be so paranoid."

"Sam," said Jessica, trying to stay calm, "I am *not* paranoid. But Paula is trying to sabotage me somehow. You've got to believe me!"

"Sabotage, Jess? Aren't you being a little melodramatic? How is Paula trying to sabotage you?"

"I don't know!" Jessica screamed. "I just know she is!" The evening was balmy, but Jessica shivered. She looked up at Sam and continued in a quiet voice, "It's bad enough that my sister and all my friends are on Paula's side. Now you're on her side, too."

"This isn't about taking sides, Jess."

"Then why is sticking up for her more important to you than I am?"

"Jessica, you're making me angry now. And I see what's going on. Your little protégé is ready

104

to make her own friends, and you can't handle that."

Sam stalked away, but halfway across the parking lot he turned around and yelled back at her, "What do you want, Jess? To control Paula? She's not your puppet, you know!"

"No," whispered Jessica. "But I may be hers."

Nine

"Here it is!" said Elizabeth, thumbing through Tuesday morning's *Sweet Valley News*. "We're the lead story on the entertainment page!"

Elizabeth was in the *Oracle* office during study hall. Enid, Annie, Robin, and Penny were with her. All of them were helping with the publicity for the play.

"Hey, your article looks great!" said Enid, looking over her shoulder. "Congratulations, Liz."

"I can't believe it," said Annie. "Out of all the photos the cast posed for, the newspaper decided to run one of us witches! It's not every day that I get my picture in the paper—even if I am in the background, behind Lila. She really makes a creepy-looking witch!"

"Well, it's a wonderful photo, and great publicity for the play," said Penny.

"I bet Lila isn't thrilled about it," said Enid.

"I don't know if she's seen the newspaper yet," said Annie, grinning. "But I sure wouldn't want to be the one to show it to her."

The door opened and a handcart loaded with cardboard boxes bumped into the office. Winston and Olivia came in behind it, Winston pushing the cart.

"Here are a few tons of stuff from the printers," he said. "And they're addressed to a Ms. Wakefield, Queen of Publicity!"

"The posters!" cried Elizabeth. "I can't wait to see them!"

"Neither could I," said Olivia, grinning.

Elizabeth saw that one of the boxes had already been torn open. With a flourish, Winston pulled out a poster and placed it in Elizabeth's hands.

"That looks wonderful!" Elizabeth exclaimed. "Your design has just the right eerie sort of feeling, Olivia. You should keep a few for yourself."

"Now comes the hard part," said Olivia. "We've got to put these up all over town today!"

Robin picked up a clipboard. "Elizabeth and I have divided the town into different areas. We'll assign a stack of posters and a neighborhood to each person on the publicity committee."

"Robin, you can add Paula Perrine to the list of people who are putting up posters," Elizabeth said. "She asked me if she could take care of some of them for us. I can't believe how eager she always is to help out!" She began opening the boxes of programs. "Mr. Goodman told me that Paula even helped the judges with the paperwork when they were choosing the winning poster," Elizabeth continued. "She was so quiet about the whole thing that even I didn't know she was helping them—Paula never wants any recognition for anything she does. But Mr. Goodman said she was invaluable."

"Have you received a reply from the *Los Angeles Times* reviewer?" Penny asked Elizabeth.

"Not yet, but I'm expecting to hear something definite by tomorrow," said Elizabeth. "I did speak to Cynthia Chang yesterday. She's the arts critic for the *Sweet Valley News*, and she said she'll definitely be there on opening night to review the play. In fact, all of the papers that have gotten back to me so far have said they'll send reviewers opening night. So will *L.A. Arts* magazine."

"Why are they all coming on opening night?" asked Winston. "Wouldn't it make more sense for them to wait until we've had a little more practice and really know what we're doing? What if we bomb?"

"Newspapers like to review a play as early as possible so that people who read the review will have time to get tickets," Elizabeth explained. "That means we've got to get the reviewers to come to the first performance, or they won't come at all. But it sounds as if that won't be a problem —we're going to have an audience full of critics that night!"

"Then they're going to have to fight for seats," Robin pointed out. "Tickets are going like crazy, even without the posters up."

"Publicity around school has been great," said

Penny. "I think we'll be sold out for opening night this Friday—and maybe for Saturday's performance, too. If you haven't all picked up tickets for your families, you'd better get them now."

"Are there still tickets left for the second week?" asked Annie. "My mom can't make it to opening night. She'll be out of town this weekend."

"You're still OK for next week," said Robin. "But I wouldn't wait until the last minute to buy tickets."

"The Wakefield family and friends will be part of the opening night crowd," said Elizabeth. "Jessica made sure of that! My parents, Todd, Steven, Sam, and I will all be in the audience, cheering her on."

"I'm glad to hear that Sam's still coming," Annie told her. "Jessica said things have been strained between them since she walked out on him at the Dairi Burger Friday." She hesitated for a moment before going on. "Actually, Liz, I'm a little worried about Jessica. Has she seemed . . . well, *unreasonable* to you lately?"

"How could you tell?" Penny asked dryly.

"I know she's been putting in a lot of work on this play, Liz," Annie continued, "but lately she's been almost like a different person. Even Lila and Amy are sick of her. She loses her temper over little things. And she's awfully weird around Paula. It's as though she's jealous that Paula has become popular. But I can't believe that someone as popular as Jessica—"

"No, that couldn't be it," Elizabeth broke in loyally. "It's probably just an attack of the jitters.

109

I think Jessica is a lot more nervous about opening night than she's letting on to any of us."

"But why would she single out Paula to abuse?" Annie persisted. "She goes to pieces whenever Paula's around—snapping at her one minute and apologizing the next. And when Paula's not around, Jessica seems obsessed with her."

Elizabeth knew Annie was right. Jessica did seem jealous of Paula. *No*, thought Elizabeth. *It was more than jealousy. Jessica actually seems afraid of Paula. But that doesn't make sense. What does Jessica have to be afraid of?*

"Maybe she picks on Paula because she knows Paula is the only one who'll put up with it," suggested Enid, breaking in on Elizabeth's thoughts.

"You've got a point there," said Annie. "No matter how fed up everyone else is with Jessica's stardom act, Paula always sticks up for her."

"I think Jessica should be grateful," said Enid, pulling a stack of programs from a box. "She's lucky to have a friend as loyal as Paula."

"Oh no!" cried Lila that night, putting down her spoon. "There's another one!" She pointed to the *Macbeth* poster on the wall of the ice cream parlor. "That's not what I want to face after a hard evening of power shopping. I will never forgive Elizabeth Wakefield for as long as I live! How did she get those things up all over town so quickly?"

Paula shrugged. "She must have had a lot of help."

"They're not that bad, Lila," said Amy. She sipped her ice-cream soda. "I think you make a really scary witch."

"Thanks a lot," snapped Lila. "That has certainly always been my life's ambition."

"You can hardly blame Elizabeth," Paula pointed out. "She's just doing her job." She made a face. "At least she didn't get them to pick a design that featured Jessica looking melodramatic."

Lila raised her eyebrows. *Paula's got more backbone than I realized*, she thought. "I didn't think I'd ever hear any criticism of Jessica Wakefield from *you*!" she said. "But you're right. Jessica's head is too swelled up as it is. And they call *us* the weird sisters!" She sighed. "I don't have much use for either Wakefield twin right now. I can't believe Elizabeth would send the newspaper a photograph like that of me."

"I never would have guessed that you were upset about that photo," Amy said sarcastically. "You've only complained about it three hundred times today."

"I have a right to be upset. And I'm sick of this whole witch thing. I just can't stand it anymore!"

"Aren't you being a little overdramatic?" asked Amy.

"I don't think so," Lila fumed. "All of my friends will see those pictures!"

"You wouldn't drop out of the play at this point, would you?" asked Paula.

"No," said Lila. "But I swear I'm going to do

111

everything I can to keep people from associating me with a witch." A slow smile spread across her face. "They'll hardly even know I'm onstage."

"Double, double, toil and trouble," said Amy. "Methinks you're cooking up some scheme. What are you going to do?"

"You'll find out soon enough," Lila said mysteriously. "Let's just say that opening night may hold a few surprises for everyone."

Paula stared intently at the *Macbeth* poster on the wall. "I'm sure it will be a night to remember," she said.

Elizabeth left the *Oracle* office after study hall the next morning and started down the hallway.

"Paula!" she said. "I almost walked right past you! Were you waiting for me? You didn't have to stand out in the hallway. You could've come into the office."

"Oh no," Paula insisted. "I was just walking by. I didn't even know you had study hall."

"Really? It would seem that you *did* know," Elizabeth said, amused. She resumed walking, and Paula fell into step. "I mean, I *did* just come from my study hall period, but I didn't say anything about it."

Paula blushed. "I guess Jessica told me you spend study hall at the newspaper a lot of the time," she said quickly. "So I just assumed when I saw you coming out of there—"

"It's OK, Paula," Elizabeth assured her. "You don't have to explain. In fact, I'm glad I ran into you. Can you do me a favor?"

112

"Anything, Elizabeth. Anything at all."

"I just spoke to the *L.A. Times* entertainment editor," Elizabeth said. "And we're getting a reviewer on opening night!"

Paula stopped walking. "That's fantastic!" she breathed.

Elizabeth smiled at the expression on the other girl's face. "I guess you're as excited about this as I am, Paula. It's great the way everyone at school has gotten so caught up in this production—and you've been one of the most supportive!"

"Oh, I'm always that way when it comes to the theatre," Paula said, her eyes shining. She continued quickly, "But mostly I'm happy about the *Times* reviewer because I know how thrilled Jessica will be to hear the news."

"Actually, that's what I wanted to ask you about," Elizabeth said. "I won't see Jessica in class until late this afternoon. And I'll be busy with Mr. Goodman all through lunch. Jessica will want to know all about the review as soon as possible. Would you tell her for me that it's all set?"

"Of course, Elizabeth," Paula promised. "In fact, I'll see her at her locker in just a few minutes. I'll tell her right away."

"Thanks, Paula," said Elizabeth. "I owe you one."

"No you don't," Paula answered seriously. "You don't owe me a thing."

"So what kind of food do all of you think we should have at my cast party?" asked Lila at lunch that day.

Jessica wondered why she had bothered to eat with her old friends that day. She was sitting directly across the table from Lila, but Lila was looking only at Amy and Paula for suggestions.

"Let's concoct some sort of fruit punch," suggested Paula. "We could call it witches' brew."

"That's a great idea," said Lila.

"Speaking of witches," said Amy, "where's Annie today?"

"She had a last-minute costume fitting," Paula explained. Jessica wondered how Paula had known. She herself hadn't heard anything about another fitting for Annie. She picked up her oatmeal cookie and concentrated on nibbling at it.

"What about finger food?"

"*Finger* food?" asked Amy. "Is that anything like your pilot's thumb?"

Lila groaned. "Don't remind me," she said.

"Opening night is two days away, Lila," Amy said. "You can't deny your witchiness forever, you know."

"Oh yes I can," said Lila ominously. "In fact, I'm trying not to think about the play at all."

She's not the only one, thought Jessica.

Lila's tone brightened. "Parties are much more fun!" she said. "When Friday's performance is over, I plan to change into that fabulous dress I bought last night, and forget all about pilot's thumbs, filthy air, and rats without tails."

"As soon as you come out in that beautiful blue dress, Lila," said Paula, "everyone at the cast party will forget about the play."

Jessica dropped her oatmeal cookie. "What blue dress?" she asked sharply.

"I told you," Lila said, "the one I bought last night."

"Lila, Paula, and I went to the mall last night," Amy explained, peeling an orange. "She found this great cornflower-blue dress at Bibi's."

"You should see it, Jessica!" Paula raved. "It's pure silk, and slinky, with little buttons—"

"The three of you went shopping last night?" Jessica asked incredulously. *She* was the one who usually went shopping with Lila and Amy. "What else did you do?"

"Nothing much," said Amy, shrugging her shoulders. "We shopped for a while, and then we got an ice cream at Casey's."

"Not that it's any of *your* business," Lila added.

"Oh, we're sorry, Jessica," Paula said sweetly. "You're feeling left out, aren't you? Of course, we would have *loved* to have you with us."

Jessica saw Lila roll her eyes at Amy. She suddenly didn't feel like eating anymore.

"But we knew you'd want to rehearse last night," Paula continued. "Plus you really need your sleep. You said you've been having trouble sleeping lately. But that's not surprising—we all know how hard you've been working."

"Yes," Jessica forced herself to say. "I *was* busy rehearsing all night."

"So, Paula," asked Amy, "have you decided if you're going back to Lisette's to buy that white dress you tried on? It would be great for the cast party."

115

"I did love it," Paula admitted. "But I can't imagine spending that kind of money on one dress."

"I'll put it on my father's credit card for you," said Lila. "He'll never know the difference."

Now I've heard everything, Jessica thought. Lila and Jessica had been best friends for ages, and Lila had never offered to buy *her* a dress.

"You should get the dress, Paula," Amy urged. "It makes you look so glamorous—like a real actress!"

Paula beamed. "Thank you, Amy," she said. "And thanks for the offer, Lila. I'll think about it."

"How about you, Lady Wakefield?" asked Amy. "What are you wearing to the cast party? You've been awfully quiet—or is it just that we serfs aren't worthy of your royal attention?"

"I'm just a little nervous, I guess," Jessica said, smiling weakly.

"With your talent, you don't need to be nervous, Jessica," Paula reassured her. "But it's only natural, as modest as you are. After all, with a real theatre critic from the *L.A. Times* coming Friday night—"

"Well, we *hope* the paper will send someone," corrected Jessica. "But Elizabeth told me in homeroom today that she still hasn't heard for sure."

"Oh, didn't you know?" said Paula. "Elizabeth got a call during study hall this morning. It's all set. A reviewer is coming from the *Times*, as well as from all the other papers she contacted."

"That's funny," Jessica mused. "Elizabeth hasn't said a word about it to me." *Paula seems to be talking to a lot of people behind my back these days,*

116

she thought. "You'd think she would have told her own twin. She *knows* how anxious I am about the reviews."

"Now don't go getting all weird on us again," Lila warned. "She probably just hasn't run into you since she found out."

Jessica took a sip of her milk. She was trying to fight down a feeling of rising panic. "Yes, I guess you're right," she said lightly. "I'm sure Liz has been searching all over for me, trying to tell me the good news."

It was bad enough that Paula was stealing Sam and all of Jessica's girlfriends. Now she was taking away Elizabeth, too. And nobody believed Jessica when she tried to tell them what was happening.

Jessica glanced quickly at Paula. She was sure she saw a satisfied little smile playing around the corners of Paula's mouth. Jessica looked away. *The worst thing about it*, she thought, *is that there's nothing I can do to stop her.*

"Come, you spirits that tend on mortal thoughts, unsex me here," called Jessica, onstage in Thursday's dress rehearsal.

The speech was a dark, ominous one, and Jessica was losing herself in it. "And fill me, from the crown to the toe, top-full of direst cruelty!" she entreated. She was steeling herself for the terrible deed she had made up her mind to do in order to fulfill her ambition of setting her husband on the throne. As she spoke tension mounted in the room.

"Make thick my blood, stop up the access and passage to remorse, that no compunctious visitings of nature shake my fell purpose . . ."

Then something about the words she had been reciting made her feel panicky, and Jessica realized that she was thinking of Paula.

She was sure that Paula had some kind of "fell purpose" of her own, but what was it? Jessica shuddered, suddenly remembering Steven's words about *Macbeth* being a cursed play.

When Jessica finished her monologue, a spontaneous burst of applause made her jump. She knew that she had never done the speech better. She felt strangely exhilarated—and just plain strange. On one level, she was completely focused on the character and the scene. But at the same time, her mind kept wandering all over the place.

She wondered if Sam was still mad at her. She had talked to him several times since Friday, but he had been awfully short with her. And she didn't deserve it. *He* was the one who had been flirting with Paula at the Dairi Burger.

Jessica hadn't seen Sam since that night. She hoped Paula hadn't, either. *But I'm not going to think about that now*, she told herself.

Bill entered, with a light-colored beard pasted on his tanned face. Close up, it looked pretty silly, Jessica thought. She fought a hysterical urge to laugh, but she knew the beard would look real from the audience's perspective.

The audience. That was where Mr. Goodman was sitting right at that moment. The director was out there in the dark with Mr. Cooper, the faculty advisors, Elizabeth, and some of the crew members.

She and Bill continued with the scene. She knew they were performing it perfectly. When she exited the stage a few minutes later, Jessica's eyes were wet with tears.

"Great work, Jessica!" whispered the assistant director to her backstage. "The intensity you brought to that monologue was as good as a professional!"

"Thanks, Frank," she mumbled. Several other cast and crew members congratulated her, but Jessica barely noticed. She fidgeted behind the curtain, waiting for her next cue—Macbeth's line about "vaulting ambition."

Again, she found herself thinking of Paula. Where was Paula, anyhow? As much as she hated being around her lately, it was worse not to know where Paula was—or who Paula was with.

Forty minutes later, Jessica breathed a sigh of relief at the opening of act four. She had been so focused on her part that she'd hardly noticed what was going on in the play when it wasn't her turn onstage. Her surroundings didn't even seem real.

But now she knew she would have a few minutes to collect her thoughts before she had to put on her nightgown for her final scene—the sleep-walking scene at the start of act five.

From behind the curtain, she watched while Lila, Annie, and Rosa hobbled onstage for the "double, double, toil, and trouble" scene.

"This is fantastic!" whispered Winston, coming up behind Jessica. As usual, she laughed at the sight of his knobby knees in the orange tights that were part of his costume.

"You are fantastic!" he raved. "Bill is fantastic! The sets are fantastic! Even Lila Fair-is-Fowler is fantastic! And of course it goes without saying that yours truly is fantastic!"

He did a little jig that made her laugh even more. Then he continued, still whispering, "A lot of theatre people swear that a good dress rehearsal means a lousy performance. If that's true, we are going to bomb big-time tomorrow—because tonight, Lady M., we are incredible!"

"Shhh!" Frank quieted them. He pointed at Winston. "Banquo's ghost—get ready to go on!"

Jessica put her hand over her mouth to stifle a giggle. Winston bowed formally and then scurried to the curtain to await his cue.

Jessica stood alone backstage. She heard thunder. For a moment, she wondered how Emily Mayer had produced such a realistic sound effect. Then she realized that the thunder was outside, and that it was still distant. Was a thunderstorm unlucky? Maybe the storm was part of the *Macbeth* curse.

Jessica shuddered. She knew that the weather reports had been forecasting rain. It was supposed to hold off until the next day, but the air outside already felt thick and oppressive. Even backstage, Jessica felt as if she were suffocating. Suddenly, she was terrified.

Ten

"What if Steven's right?" Jessica asked Prince Albert as she entered the living room. "What if *Macbeth* really *is* a cursed play? What if I fall flat on my face tonight? What if I forget my lines?"

The golden Labrador tilted his head and looked at her quizzically. She sat on the couch and absentmindedly began stroking the dog's back.

"It's pouring outside, Prince Albert. That's got to be bad luck on opening night. It never rains in Sweet Valley; it must be the *Macbeth* curse."

She jumped up and ran to the window. The overcast sky looked a lot like the one DeeDee had designed for the backdrop of the witches' scenes.

"I know I'm being silly," Jessica said, walking back toward the dog. "But I wish someone were here with me. Mom and Dad are still at work. Sam isn't even coming here before he goes to the

121

play. But why isn't Elizabeth home yet? School let out early today because of opening night. She should have been home hours ago!"

Jessica raced into the kitchen to check the time. It was almost five o'clock. Where *was* Elizabeth?

Thunder crashed outside. Jessica watched from the doorway as Prince Albert tried, unsuccessfully, to burrow under the couch. "Stop being such a weenie," she told the dog—and herself.

Suddenly she remembered what Elizabeth had told her. "You can stop worrying about Elizabeth, pooch," she called across the room. "She's staying after school to put together press kits for the reviewers who are coming tonight—reviewers who are coming to write about me!" Elizabeth had said that Todd would drive her home after basketball practice. Elizabeth would quickly change her clothes, and then the twins would drive to the play together.

She raced back to the living room, crouched on the carpet beside the dog, and asked him seriously, "What if I get bad reviews? How will I ever face everyone again?"

Prince Albert didn't answer.

"Panicking won't do any good," Jessica told herself. She laughed nervously. "Neither will talking to a dog. Practicing my lines—that's what would help." She stood up and struck a pose from act three, scene four. She opened her mouth—and her mind went blank. She couldn't remember the scene at all. In fact, she couldn't remember a single line from any of her scenes.

"Oh no!" she gasped, sinking to the carpet. She closed her eyes and leaned her head against the side of the couch. How could she go onstage in a few hours if she couldn't remember her lines? Opening night would be a disaster. Her chance to be a star was ruined.

Suddenly, the lines from act two, scene two popped into her head. She jumped up and recited them.

"That which hath made them drunk hath made me bold," she said stoutly. "What hath quenched them hath given me fire."

Jessica sighed with relief. It was good that the words she had remembered first were about having gotten up her courage. She needed courage as badly as Lady Macbeth did. She really did know her lines, Jessica told herself for the tenth time that day. Now she could remember them all. And she could still say them just as well as she'd said them in dress rehearsal on Thursday. The *Macbeth* curse didn't apply to her.

The phone rang, and Jessica jumped. She chided herself for being so antsy and reached for the receiver.

"Jessica, is that you?"

Jessica tensed. The voice was Paula's.

"Hello, Jess?"

Jessica swallowed. Paula was the last person she wanted to talk to, but she couldn't deny the terror she heard in the girl's voice. Something was really wrong.

"Yes, Paula," she said in a low voice. "It's me."

"Jessica!" Paula pleaded on the phone. "I need your help. I don't know what to do, and you're the only person I really trust."

"Paula," said Jessica, "you sound far away. Stop crying and tell me where you are and what's wrong."

"I'm sorry to be such a baby, but I'm so scared, Jessica."

"What happened? Where are you?"

"I'm at a gas station in Cold Springs, calling from a pay phone. Jessica, it's my father," she said, and began to cry again.

Through the phone, Jessica heard a crash of thunder in the background at the same time as she heard it outside her own window. Paula stifled a nervous scream. Jessica's heart went out to the girl. As upset as she had allowed herself to get about the play, she knew that her own troubles were trivial compared to Paula's. She knew how terrified Paula was of her abusive father.

"I got a call last night from Ed Kronwitz," Paula explained tearfully. "He's a mean, awful man; he plays poker with my father. He said my father was in the hospital here and that I should come fast. It sounded really serious, Jess. I didn't know what to do. I couldn't tell the people I'm living with. They're friends of my mother's, and they would never have let me go to him."

"But Paula, I thought you were afraid of your father. Why would you want to go see him?"

"It must be hard for you to understand. Your own family is so wonderful. I hate my father, Jessica, I really do. But he's still my father and

124

he doesn't have anyone else now. I thought he was sick. So I took a bus here to see him; that's why I wasn't in school today. But Jessica, the whole thing was a lie!" Paula's voice had reached a terrible pitch.

"Calm down, Paula. What do you mean?"

"He wasn't in the hospital at all. He was perfectly fine—just drunk. He wanted money, and he said I'd have to stay and live with him from now on! I sneaked away this afternoon, but he took all the money I'd brought with me for the return bus trip." Paula paused. "Jessica," she said after a moment, "I'm stranded here. I know the first performance is tonight, but what if my father comes looking for me? What if he finds me and drags me back with him? I need your help! Will you come get me?"

Jessica hesitated for only a second. "Of course I'll come, Paula. The curtain doesn't go up until seven o'clock. That should give me just enough time to pick you up and get us both over to the school. I'll leave a note asking Liz to tell Mr. Goodman I'll be there around curtain time. I don't have to be dressed and onstage until scene five." She reached for a pencil and picked up a piece of junk mail to write on. "OK, Paula. Give me directions to where you are."

"Jessica!" called Elizabeth from the bottom of the stairs. The only answer was a roar of thunder from outside the house.

That's strange, thought Elizabeth. Her twin didn't seem to be at home. No wonder the Jeep

125

wasn't in the driveway. With the curtain going up in an hour, Jessica should have been ready to drive over to school by now. Her twin was so excited about this play that Elizabeth couldn't believe she would take any chances on missing opening night.

"Where could she be?" she asked Prince Albert. Normally, Elizabeth would have called Lila or Amy to ask about her sister, but that seemed pointless. Outside of school and rehearsals, Jessica had spent hardly any time with her old friends lately. And Sam would be on his way to Sweet Valley for the performance by now.

"If you were Jessica, who would you be with?" she asked the dog. "I know—Paula!"

As a member of the production staff, Elizabeth had a copy of the director's cast list. She pulled it from her book bag, found Paula's home phone number, and dialed it.

"Hello, this is the Perrine residence," said a pleasant female voice.

Elizabeth was confused. Paula had said she was living with friends of her mother.

"Uh, does Paula Perrine live there?" she asked. "I'm Elizabeth Wakefield, one of her friends from Sweet Valley High."

"Well, hello, dear. I've heard a lot about you. How sweet of you to call," said the woman. "I'm Paula's mother. You know, we've been here for more than a month, but I haven't had a chance to meet any of Paula's new friends. I don't know why she hasn't invited some of you girls over."

Elizabeth didn't know what to say. But Mrs. Perrine was talkative enough for both of them.

"I'm so sorry, Elizabeth," she went on cheerfully. "Paula's not home right now. Her brother, Marty, took her to the mall to do some last-minute shopping for the performance tonight. She said she found the perfect dress for the cast party. I'm so proud of Paula for playing the lead!"

Elizabeth's head was spinning. The lead? And what about Paula's dead mother and her runaway brother? What about her abusive father? Well, there was one way to find out the truth, Elizabeth decided.

She asked, "Does that mean that you and Mr. Perrine will be attending the play tonight?"

"Oh, I'll be there with Marty, of course. But the children's father died more than ten years ago. I'm surprised Paula never mentioned it. Well, I'm sure you'll want to get ready for the play now, so I won't keep you any longer. It was so nice chatting with you, dear. I'll tell Paula you called."

"Uh, don't bother," Elizabeth said quietly. "I have a feeling I'll see her tonight."

As she hung up the phone Elizabeth thought of the lies Paula had been telling everyone. Only Jessica had suspected that Paula was hiding something, and no one—not even her own sister —had believed her. A loud clap of thunder made Elizabeth jump. Now Jessica was missing.

Jessica thought she would go crazy if that noisy windshield wiper blade didn't stop squeaking.

She turned off the wipers, but then water streamed down the glass so heavily that she couldn't see through it. She flipped the wipers back on and squinted through the falling rain.

"Elm Street," she read aloud from a street sign. "But there's not supposed to be an Elm Street!" she wailed. "This is the third right. It should be Henderson Avenue!"

This wasn't getting her anywhere. She consulted the directions Paula had given her. Maybe she had miscounted the intersections. Maybe she still had one street to go. The next corner had to be Henderson.

She nearly missed the intersection in the rain. She screeched to a stop and backed up to read the street sign. A horn blared behind her as thunder crashed nearby. Jessica jumped. Yellow headlights shone very close behind, appearing spidery through her rain-splattered back window. The other car pulled around her and drove on, honking angrily.

"Why can't they make street signs easier to read?" she asked tearfully. The windows of the Jeep were fogging up so badly that she could barely see out. She rolled down her window and peered through the rapidly growing darkness, ignoring the splash of water on her face. This *had* to be Henderson Avenue.

"Faulkner Street!"

She had to face it: she was lost, and she had been for the last half-hour. Paula was in trouble and Jessica couldn't find her. It was almost six-thirty and she was somewhere in Cold Springs, an hour from Sweet Valley. The opening night curtain would go up at seven.

Another loud crash of thunder made her jump. "Steven was right!" she said aloud, sobbing. "This play is cursed." Then she remembered something else. She had forgotten to leave a note telling Elizabeth where she was. She pounded both fists on the steering wheel and was startled by a blast from her own horn.

"Why am I such an airhead?" she asked herself. "Elizabeth wouldn't have run off without telling anyone. And Elizabeth never would have gotten herself lost."

But was it really Jessica's fault? There had to have been something wrong with Paula's directions. Maybe Paula had been so upset that she'd made a mistake.

No, Jessica realized. Nobody could give directions that bad.

Not unless she was doing it on purpose.

Thinking of Elizabeth gave Jessica an idea. Her sensible sister always carried a map in the glove compartment. She jerked the car to the side of the road, pulled out the map, and frantically unfolded it.

The windshield wipers were squeaking again. "Shut up!" she yelled. She switched them off again.

Jessica scanned the map by the watery light of a nearby street lamp. Her suspicions were right. Paula's directions had led her on a wild goose chase. Paula had tricked her to make Jessica miss opening night.

"Paula's a better actress than I thought," she

said to herself quietly. Then she began to sob again. "Why didn't anyone *believe* me?"

Jessica wanted to lean her head on the steering wheel and cry, but she wasn't ready to give up—not yet. She saw a lit phone booth a block ahead. She would call Mr. Goodman and get him to hold the curtain. She would make tonight's performance if it was the last thing she ever did!

"Mr. Goodman!" she yelled into the phone a few minutes later. "It's Jessica Wakefield. There's been a problem—sort of an emergency."

"Ms. Wakefield!" said the director. "I had expected to see you here by now."

"I'm sorry, Mr. Goodman. It's a long story; I'll explain later. But I'll be there in less than an hour. I'm not in the first few scenes anyway. You'll need to hold the curtain for only fifteen minutes or so. Can you do that?"

"I'm afraid the show must go on as scheduled, Ms. Wakefield. But don't worry. Just get here as soon as you can. Your understudy has saved the day. Paula is already in costume and ready to go on."

Eleven

Elizabeth left her post at the stage door and walked to the back of the crowded auditorium. She squeezed past Todd and sat beside him, staring at the empty seat to her left.

"Well, she hasn't shown up, and there's only a few more minutes until curtain time," she said quietly.

"Don't worry, Elizabeth," Todd said, taking her hand. "You heard what Mr. Goodman said. She called more than half an hour ago, and she's fine. She'll be here soon."

"Not soon enough to be in tonight's performance," whispered Sam. He was sitting on the other side of the seat they had saved for Jessica. He made a face. "It's a good thing her understudy is here and ready to go on," he said sarcastically.

131

"Thanks for coming back to my house so quickly when I called you after I talked to Paula's mother," Elizabeth told Todd. "I don't know what I would've done if I'd been alone. I almost called the police."

"It wouldn't have been the end of the world if you had," Todd reassured her. "But it did make more sense to come here first to see if she was already backstage."

"I know," Elizabeth acknowledged. "And if we hadn't, we wouldn't have heard from Frank that Mr. Goodman had already talked to Jessica."

Relieved to know that her sister was safe, Elizabeth had explained the situation to her parents and Sam as soon as they had arrived at the school. Now the rest of the Wakefield family was sitting in their reserved seats up front. Elizabeth, Todd, and Sam were near the back door, where they could see Jessica when she showed up.

"I feel so terrible!" Elizabeth whispered, trying to blink back tears. "Jessica told me Paula was up to something, and I didn't take her seriously."

"You're not the only one," said Sam. "I thought Jess was worrying for nothing. Paula seemed so harmless. Speaking of Lady Understudy, did you manage to talk to her backstage?"

"No," said Elizabeth. "I couldn't even get close to her, with all those makeup and costume people around her. And Mr. Goodman was going crazy about some problem with the dry ice. I couldn't get to him to tell him what happened."

The house lights began to dim.

"I can't believe that Paula is going to get away with this!" Elizabeth said tearfully.

"Don't worry," Sam whispered. "I have a feeling the truth will come out before the night is over."

Jessica slipped into the auditorium through the back door and stood in the dark for a minute.

"I have no spur to prick the sides of my intent," said Bill, onstage as Macbeth, "but only vaulting ambition . . ."

She noticed Elizabeth, Todd, and Sam in the back row just as her sister spotted her. Jessica slid past Todd and Elizabeth to the seat they had saved for her, and saw Paula walking onstage.

"What happened?" Elizabeth asked her sister.

"Not now," Jessica whispered back, her gaze riveted on the stage. This scene contained some of her best speeches—except that they were *Paula's* speeches now.

"Was the hope drunk wherein you dressed yourself?" Paula asked. "Hath it slept since?"

Jessica felt as if Lady Macbeth were speaking directly to her, chastising her for missing her big chance to fulfill her own ambition. *If only I hadn't been so "full of the milk of human kindness" when Paula called with her sob story!* she thought wryly.

As Paula spoke her voice grew darker and more powerful.

"The little serpent does a great Lady Macbeth," Jessica admitted under her breath. Paula's Lady Macbeth was positively chilling—majestic, determined, and cruel. But it still wasn't as incredible as Paula's offstage act had been.

Jessica watched the rest of the play with a strange mix of emotions. She was both mesmerized and sickened by Paula's performance. There was no denying that Paula was a very good actress. Still, Jessica desperately wanted to be onstage herself.

Finally, the last curtain fell.

"Let's not wait around for the curtain calls," Elizabeth whispered. "Paula's real encore is coming at the cast party."

Jessica nodded solemnly, and the four slipped out the back of the auditorium before the house lights came up.

"I'll see you inside in a few minutes, after you park the car," said Elizabeth. "Sam and Jessica must have been held up at the last red light. They should be along any minute." She waved as Todd pulled away in his BMW.

Elizabeth had told Jessica the truth about Paula's family as they left the school. Now she stopped for a minute outside the Fowler mansion, watching for her sister, but eventually she decided to wait for her inside. She could already hear music and laughter resonating from the party room.

She slipped into the room unnoticed and blinked for a few moments in the bright lights of the crystal chandeliers. Around her, she could hear people discussing Paula's powerful performance.

134

"Elizabeth!"

She turned to see Cynthia Chang walking toward her with a camera around her neck. "Hi, Cynthia," Elizabeth said absently, hoping her smile didn't look too forced. "Did you get some good material for your review in the *Sweet Valley News*?"

"The play was excellent!" answered the young reporter. "In fact, I'd say it was the best high school production I've ever seen. I'm so glad you suggested that I attend. Bill Chase is a real professional—he was even better tonight than he was in *Splendor in the Grass*."

"Oh, yes," murmured Elizabeth. "We're all proud of Bill." She could see Bill on the other side of the room, talking with Mr. Goodman while the two accepted congratulations.

"But the real surprise of the evening was the girl who played Lady Macbeth, Paula Perrine!" Cynthia raved. "It's hard to believe she was only the understudy. Her performance was awesome, in the true sense of the word."

"Yes," said Elizabeth. "Nobody ever imagined that Paula would turn out to be such a convincing Lady Macbeth."

Cynthia didn't seem to notice her acid tone. "I saw in the program that Jessica Wakefield was supposed to play the lead," the reviewer said. "Isn't she your sister? I hope she's not seriously ill."

"Oh, no," said Elizabeth. "In fact, I think Jessica will be feeling a lot better really soon."

"Here comes Paula now," said Cynthia. "If

you'll excuse me, I'd like to get a few photos of her." She scurried toward the center of the room, where a crowd was gathering.

Wild applause started as more people caught sight of Paula, who was promenading in on the arm of Frank O'Donnell. Flashbulbs lit up her dazzling smile. Her silky hair was drawn up into a sleek French twist, and she carried an armful of long-stemmed roses against the bodice of her strapless, full-skirted white dress. Elizabeth knew that the dress must have cost a fortune.

As Elizabeth watched, Lila greeted Paula warmly and the two began laughing together as though they were best friends. It bothered Elizabeth to see Paula taking her sister's place with her friends. *Jessica suspected this betrayal*, Elizabeth remembered guiltily. *And I didn't believe her.*

An angry urge to confront Paula rose in Elizabeth, but she fought it down. This was Jessica's battle, not hers. She sidled up closer to hear what was being said—careful, though, to stay out of Paula's line of sight.

"Paula, you were wonderful!" said Amy Sutton, pushing through the crowd and hugging the sophomore. "It's hard to believe that someone as sweet and shy as you are could be so good at playing a ruthless, ambitious villain!"

Paula smiled graciously. "Thank you, Amy. I'm just glad I had the chance to try." She set down the bouquet of roses to accept a glass of sparkling cider from a uniformed waiter.

"Your parents must be very proud," said Cynthia Chang, snapping a photograph as she edged through the crowd.

"Yes," said Paula. "My mother is just thrilled!"

Elizabeth noticed a flicker of confusion on Lila's face. But then Winston whispered something in Lila's ear and she turned to stick her tongue out at him, obviously forgetting about Paula's family for the time being.

"Paula, your performance was incredible!" breathed Annie. "But I still can't imagine what would have kept Jessica away. She was so excited about this play."

"She called me this afternoon and said she had some errand to run in Cold Springs," Paula lied. Everybody in the room turned to listen. "She said she might not be back in time for the curtain," Paula went on. "I guess Jessica just didn't care very much about the play after all." Paula took a long drink of the sparkling cider, and then continued loudly, "You know how flighty she can be."

Everyone else laughed. Elizabeth was repulsed. She was relieved to feel Todd's hand on her shoulder.

"I'm here," he whispered. "And so is Jessica."

She followed his gaze and saw her sister entering quietly through a side door, with Sam right behind her. No doubt she had heard Paula's last remark. Elizabeth caught her eye, and Jessica nodded resolutely, placing a finger to her lips.

"I always knew I'd made a great Lady Macbeth!" Paula boasted. "I've been practicing the role all my life. It's been my dream since I was a little girl!"

Suddenly, a different voice filled the room.

"I know it was," said Jessica, striding toward her understudy. The crowd parted silently as she passed. "And you'd do anything to make that dream come true."

Paula smiled. Her expression was bland but triumphant, and Elizabeth thought her eyes looked like gray ice. Somebody turned off the music.

"Oh yes, you'd do *anything* to achieve your dream," Jessica repeated, stopping in front of Paula. "You'd pretend to be too shy to step out onstage—and then become my understudy behind my back. And then you'd lie about being in trouble to get me out of the way for tonight."

Elizabeth had never been prouder of her sister. Despite her jeans and sweatshirt, Jessica was calm and dignified—regal, even.

Paula stared back haughtily. Rings of dark eyeliner, left over from her stage makeup, made her look much older and very dramatic. Elizabeth felt as if she were watching a movie. Somehow, she thought, both actresses seemed larger than life.

Paula laughed scornfully. "You're just jealous!" she said. "You've been jealous of me from the moment I moved here."

"That's what you wanted everyone to think," said Jessica, looking steadily at her rival. "It was all part of your plan. And you convinced them, all right. That innocent act of yours was a better performance than anything we've seen tonight."

Elizabeth walked forward quietly to stand next to Sam, behind her sister. Todd followed her, took her hand, and squeezed it.

"You knew how much I wanted to play that role," said Jessica. "But you also knew that, offstage, I'd never be the Lady Macbeth you are. You knew that when it came down to it, I'd risk my ambition to help a friend in trouble—something you would never do. So you called me, crying. You said you'd been stranded by your abusive father—*your father who died ten years ago*." Jessica spoke calmly, but her voice filled the room, and it carried the ring of truth.

"Jessica Wakefield, you're as paranoid as ever," said Paula, shaking her head. Only a few people laughed this time.

Lila stepped away from Paula's side and joined the small group gathering behind Jessica. Amy and Annie slowly followed her.

"Your plan worked beautifully," continued Jessica. "You played Lady Macbeth in the opening-night performance. You won, Paula. People like you always win."

"That's the first sensible thing you've said all evening," Paula retorted. "Think about it tomorrow morning when you're reading my name in all the reviews!"

She stared at Jessica for more than a minute, and Jessica met her gaze. Then Paula swept her flowers off the table and glided out of the room. Frank O'Donnell and a few of her classmates followed her out.

As the door closed behind them Elizabeth

began clapping loudly for her sister. The room exploded into applause, and Jessica's friends rushed forward to hug her. Elizabeth caught sight of Jessica's face. She had never seen her sister look happier.

Twelve

Jessica sighed and looked around the sunlit patio the next morning at the people who were gathering at the Wakefields' house.

"It's good to know I have friends again!" she said. "I just hope Lila and Amy get here soon. I didn't realize how much I've missed them."

"They never stopped being your friends," Sam assured her. He twisted the lid off a bottle of suntan lotion and started rubbing lotion on her shoulders. "Hey, Prince Albert," he said as the golden dog nudged his side. "Go bother Elizabeth. Can't you see that I'm busy performing this delicate operation?"

Jessica laughed. Ever since the cast party the night before, she had been happier than she'd felt in weeks. Her friends liked her again, yesterday's storm had given way to today's sunshine, and she knew she looked terrific in her almost-new, strapless black bathing suit.

In fact, thought Jessica, the only thing that marred such a perfect day—besides having missed the performance the night before—was the loud creaking and bumping of furniture being loaded onto a moving van from the Beckwiths' house next door.

"Get down, Prince Albert!" Elizabeth ordered. "I'm busy! Go bother Todd." She pushed the dog toward her boyfriend, who began lazily scratching the retriever behind the ears.

"You never really *lost* your friends, Jess," Elizabeth said. "You were just too busy for them." She poured cranberry juice into glasses and handed one to her sister.

"I guess you're right, Liz. The only thing I lost was my chance for stardom. Those theatre critics won't be back for the show tonight or the performances next weekend." She sighed loudly. "Oh well—easy come, easy go. Still, I'd feel a lot better if Paula hadn't gotten such good reviews."

"You said it!" said Sam as he finished Jessica's shoulders and capped the suntan lotion bottle. "The little creep wowed all the local papers with her Lady Macbeth act—even though that didn't take much acting, in her case."

"But tonight's my turn," said Jessica happily. "And I'll wow all the people who really count."

"You certainly will!" Elizabeth agreed.

"As good as Paula was last night, Jess, I think I like your interpretation of the role better,"

Annie told her. "Paula comes across as totally evil. I think you give Lady Macbeth more depth."

Jessica smiled at her and reached out to pet Prince Albert. "As I said, I hadn't realized how much I missed my friends." She heard the sound of glass breaking next door and shook her head. "Remind me never to hire that moving company!"

"Do you know yet who your new neighbors will be?" asked Annie.

"No," said Elizabeth. "The Beckwiths just put the house on the market."

Prince Albert stood up and barked, wagging his tail. Winston was skipping across the patio toward them, pulling Maria behind him. "The *Los Angeles Times* is in!" he called. "And we got another great review!"

"You don't have to sound so happy about it," said Jessica.

"I have to admit that after what Lady Mac-Paula did, I wouldn't mind seeing the critics dump on her," Winston agreed. "Let's see—if I were a reviewer, I'd call her 'a walking shadow, a poor player that struts and frets her hour upon the stage and then is heard no more.'"

"Very original!" said Enid with a chuckle, climbing out of the pool. "But what did they really say?"

Winston handed the paper to Elizabeth. "Madame Publicity Director, will you do us the honor of reading it aloud?"

"Some publicity director I am!" said Elizabeth, opening the newspaper. "I was hoping the reviewers would hate Paula's performance."

"So what's the bad news?" asked Todd.

Elizabeth skimmed the review. "It's not too bad," she said. "The reviewer called her 'an overwhelming stage presence' and 'darkly powerful.' But listen to this: 'Bill Chase, as Macbeth, gave the most complex and harrowing performance of the evening, showing a range of emotion that is remarkable for a high school student. This is one young actor to keep an eye on.'"

"Way to go, Bill!" said Jessica. "And he deserves every word. By the way, when are he and DeeDee coming over?"

"They should be here any minute," said Todd.

"You haven't read the best part of the review!" Winston objected. He recited it by heart: "'Winston Egbert delivered an expressive and elegant performance as Banquo, while lending an unusual comic enthusiasm as Banquo's ghost.' That's me, all right—expressive and elegant."

"And unusually comic," quipped Jessica.

"Listen to this, everyone!" said Elizabeth, laughing. "'Lila Fowler's interpretation of the First Witch was secretive and sullen, providing a stark but interesting contrast to the gruesome hilarity of the other witches.'"

"Secretive and sullen!" cried Lila, stalking up behind them with Amy. "What do they mean by that? I may not have been quite as gruesome as Annie and Rosa, but I certainly showed as much hilarity!"

"No way, Fowler," said Winston. "You acted like you didn't want anyone to recognize you.

144

You kept hiding behind the scenery! You didn't do it that way in rehearsals."

"As silly as you looked in those orange tights," Lila retorted, "maybe *you* should have hidden behind something, too!"

"These are the forgeries of jealousy," quoted Winston. "You're just jealous because not everyone can wear orange as well as I can. And because I got to wear bright colors and show my legs."

Jessica was confused. "Who said anything about forgery?"

"It's a line from *A Midsummer Night's Dream*, Ms. Famous Shakespearean Actress," Elizabeth explained.

"Next time I make my debut as a famous actress, I think I'll do a play that's written in regular English," Jessica decided. "But speaking of costumes, are mine OK? They didn't make them over for Paula last night, did they?"

"Don't worry," said Lila. "Tracy pinned them up here and there, but the damage isn't permanent." She made a face. "At least you didn't have to wear a gray sack, a stringy wig, and wrinkly makeup."

"We know how much you hated the costume and makeup, Lila," said Annie. "But that's what people expect from *Macbeth*'s witches. You shouldn't have been embarrassed to show your face."

"She's right, Lila," said Amy. "You did come across as sullen and secretive."

"And I thought I would die when you made that remark onstage last night, after you said the line about the pig's blood," Annie continued. "Nobody whispers, 'Oh, gross!' in the middle of a Shakespeare performance!"

"Well, it was a gross line!" Lila complained. "Besides, the audience couldn't hear me."

"You did what?" asked Elizabeth, incredulous.

"I give up!" cried Lila. "From this minute forward, I will love being a witch. In tonight's performance, I'll be the most happily contented and hilariously gruesome witch anybody has ever seen. I'll show you all!"

"Uh-oh," said Winston. "I think I sense some dastardly plot!"

"Speaking of dastardly plots, has anyone heard from Jessica's underhanded understudy this morning?" asked Annie.

"Not a word," said Amy. "But I didn't really expect to. I still can't understand how she could lie to everyone that way. I thought she was our friend."

Prince Albert barked a greeting.

"Don't look now," said Sam, "but *our friend* is heading this way."

Sure enough, Paula was walking across the patio toward them, wearing a white silk blouse and faded, body-hugging jeans. Jessica was gratified to see the cold stares on her friends' faces.

"Hi, everyone!" Paula called cheerfully, standing at the edge of the pool. Prince Albert trotted over and began sniffing her, but Paula shoved him away. Jessica saw with some satisfaction that the dog was the only one who greeted her enthusiastically. But Paula didn't seem to notice the hostile expressions.

"Your father let me in, Elizabeth," she said, ignoring Jessica. "Isn't it a beautiful morning?"

"Hello, Paula," said Elizabeth guardedly. "To tell you the truth, I'm a little surprised that you would come here today."

"Did you see the reviews this morning?" asked Paula. "Even the *Times* loved us! My mother's already compiling the clippings in a scrapbook."

"Yes, we've heard about your mother," Lila commented.

Paula went on as though she hadn't noticed the interruption. "The scrapbook will be great to show at casting calls on Broadway," she said. "This is all so exciting!"

"I would think you'd had enough excitement last night," said Jessica. "Taking advantage of someone's friendship can be pretty exhausting."

Paula laughed. "Sour grapes, Jessica? I should have expected such a reaction from you. You're hopelessly naive about the way show business really works. Admit it, Jessica. You're jealous because I was a better Lady Macbeth last night than you'll ever be. You said it last night, Jessica—I've won. And that's all that's important. You'll never be a professional actress now."

Sam stood up, his fists clenched. "I think you should leave, Paula," he said in a tight controlled voice.

"Oh, be real, Sam," said Paula flippantly. "Wouldn't you rather spend your time with a winner?"

"He already does," Maria said.

"For your sake, Paula, I hope you do go to New York," Amy said coldly. "Because you sure aren't welcome here."

Paula looked around at them silently, and Jessica saw that their unfriendly faces had finally registered with her. Paula's expression slowly crumpled into one of surprise, confusion, and hurt. Next door, a piece of furniture fell with a loud crash.

Paula yanked her hand away from Prince Albert's wet tongue. "I don't understand," she said tearfully. "I thought you would all be happy for me."

"That's right, Paula, you *don't* understand," Jessica said quietly. She stood to face the younger girl. "These are my friends. They care about me the way we all cared about you—until we found out what you were really after, and what you would do to get it. But I can't even be mad at you now; I feel sorry for you."

"Paula, maybe you should leave now," Elizabeth said gently but firmly.

"You're all as naive as Jessica is!" Paula screamed. "You can't understand someone who isn't afraid to go after what she wants. Why don't you all just grow up?"

She turned to stalk out, but tripped over the dog and landed with a splash in the swimming pool.

Several people started laughing. But Jessica

looked at her sister for a moment, and then reached out a hand to help Paula out of the pool. Paula angrily shoved her arm away and pulled herself out. Then she ran, dripping, across the patio and into the house through the sliding glass door. A minute later, the front door slammed.

"There's knocking at the gate," murmured Jessica, quoting one of her lines from the play. "What's done cannot be undone."

Everyone was quiet for a minute. Jessica could hear the movers next door yelling to each other.

"So!" Winston called happily. "Who's up for a Lila Fowler lookalike contest?"

Lila knocked him into the pool. Then she lost her balance and fell in after him. She splashed a sparkling arc of water at Jessica, who smiled happily and jumped into the pool on top of her.

Jessica put her hand over her mouth to keep from laughing out loud. She was watching from the wings during act one of Saturday night's performance. Onstage, Lila was making good on her promise to act as though she loved being a witch.

"Sleep shall neither night nor day hang upon his penthouse lid," she said, throwing out her arms dramatically. In the process, Jessica noticed, she carefully positioned her hands directly in front of Annie and Rosa's faces.

Lila swaggered forward to center stage. Jessica knew that the blocking for this scene called for the witches to stay in the left-hand corner of the stage.

149

"He shall live a man forbid," Lila continued.
"Weary sev'nights nine times nine shall he dwindle, peak, and pine. Though his bark cannot be lost, yet it shall be tempest-tossed."

She pantomimed broadly, to show the bark—a boat—tossing on the waves. Then she posed dramatically for a moment before running back to the other witches and standing directly in front of Annie.

"Look what I have," she said.

"Show me, show me," Annie implored, stepping around her with an annoyed glare.

"Here I have a pilot's thumb," said Lila, "wracked as homeward he did come."

Then Jessica heard her whisper, "Yum, yum!"

If Annie and Rosa had been riding broomsticks, they would have fallen off them. Jessica could see them both trembling with suppressed laughter. Luckily, the audience didn't seem to notice.

Lila is gutsy, thought Jessica. *I'm lucky to have someone like her for a friend.* She felt especially grateful for *all* her friends that night, and for the way they had rallied around her the night before, when Paula's lies were exposed. Jessica was more disappointed about missing opening night than she had admitted to anyone, but she would have other chances. And unlike Paula, she still had her friends—and her self-respect. Paula couldn't take those things away from her.

Now she was about to prove that she still had her talent as well.

"Nervous?" a voice whispered in her ear. She

turned to see Winston in costume, ready to go onstage. Bill was right behind him.

"A little," she admitted. "But I've got a wonderful feeling about tonight's performance. I'm going to be the best Lady Macbeth anyone's ever seen—onstage, that is."

"We missed you last night, Jessica," said Bill.

"Thanks, Bill. Here comes your cue!" She parted the curtains to let them by. "And Winston," she whispered, "I like your orange tights."

"Jessica," whispered Elizabeth from behind her. "How do I look?"

"Not like me!" said Jessica, surprised. "That red wig really does the trick. You'd hardly know we're twins."

"Shhh!" Mr. Jaworski cautioned them.

Elizabeth threw him an apologetic look and lowered her voice. "Well, it's a good thing Mr. Goodman's makeup person was able to make me look so different. How would it look to the audience if Lady Macbeth's lady-in-waiting looked just like Lady Macbeth?"

"Elizabeth, I'm so glad you agreed to do this scene when Paula didn't show up tonight. The sleepwalking scene is my very best one, and there's no one in the world I'd rather be onstage with."

Elizabeth grinned. "Not even Luke Perry?"

"Not even Luke Perry," Jessica affirmed. "Do you know all the words?"

"I've been practicing them for the last hour. It's a good thing I've been coming to rehearsals. I think I absorbed a lot of the lines by osmosis! Luckily, the gentlewoman has only the one scene, and it isn't until the last act."

"You'll do great, Liz. I know you will."

"Thanks, Jessica. I'd better get back to practicing now. I just wanted to wish you luck before your first scene."

Elizabeth gave her sister a big hug.

"Here comes your cue," Elizabeth said. "Break a leg!"

Jessica squeezed her sister's hand. Then she let go of it and glided onstage, knowing that she was about to deliver a brilliant performance.

"Well, that's two performances down and two left to go!" said Annie a few hours later, raising a glass of diet soda in a toast.

"To Shakespeare, Jessica Wakefield, and the entire cast of *Macbeth*!" cried Sam.

Annie saw the caring way he looked at Jessica, and remembered with a pang that Tony used to look at her like that.

"And to Elizabeth Wakefield," said Todd, "the world's greatest pinch-hitting gentlewoman!"

"And to the Dairi Burger's hamburgers," added Winston, pouring ketchup on one, "without which we never would have made it through those strenuous days of endless rehearsing."

"Seriously, Jessica," said Barry, "you were great."

"He's right, Jessica. You were terrific," said Amy. "Especially in that last scene, when you were sleepwalking, carrying the candle. It gave me chills."

Winston jumped up from his seat. He got down on his knees and bowed before Jessica. "All hail to thee, Lady Macbeth! Hail!"

Jessica picked up a fork and pretended to knight him with it. Then Winston jumped up, kissed her hand, and went back to his hamburger.

Jessica seems a little quiet tonight, thought Annie. *She's probably just tired*. But Annie noted that Jessica was smiling broadly, and her eyes sparkled like sapphires.

Bill and DeeDee hurried into the restaurant and approached the group. Bill held something large and flat behind his back.

"OK, Elizabeth," he said breathlessly, "I've got it. Do you want to make the official presentation, or shall I?"

"Go right ahead, worthy thane," said Elizabeth, laughing.

"What gives?" said Jessica.

"Actually, I do!" said Bill. "From the cast and crew of *Macbeth*, I give this special token of our appreciation to Lila Fowler for hosting the cast party last night."

"Well, thank you," said Lila, pleased. "What is it?"

Bill held up the gift, and everyone hooted. It was a framed copy of Olivia's poster design, with the large drawing of Lila as a witch. Every member of the cast and crew had signed it.

Lila turned to Winston with a sour look. "No doubt this was your idea, Egbert."

"Who, me?"

"Yes, you!" said Lila. "But I guess it could be

153

worse. If I've got one of these posters hanging *in a closet* at home, that's one less poster out on the streets for other people to see!"

Several of the kids gathered around Lila to look at the poster.

"So is your mother still out of town?" Elizabeth asked Annie. "It's too bad she missed tonight's performance. She threw an amused glanced in Lila's direction. "The witch scenes were particularly interesting tonight!"

"They certainly were," Annie agreed, laughing. "And you were great as the gentlewoman! I don't know how you learned those lines so quickly." She took a drink of her soda. "Anyhow, my mom gets back from New York on Wednesday, so she'll be here for next weekend's shows. But you know, I talked to her the other night, and she says she's going back to New York again a few days later."

"It must be rough, being alone so much," Elizabeth said sympathetically.

"Oh, it hasn't been bad," said Annie. "Besides, I've been so busy with the play that I haven't had a chance to be lonely."

"At least you know that your mom's there doing something exciting," said Jessica. "Being a model must be wonderful. Maybe that should be my next ambition."

"I think we've heard enough about ambition to last us quite a while," said Robin. "Besides, we're expecting you back on the cheerleading squad in time for the basketball tournament at Big Mesa."

"Never fear," said Jessica. "Lady Wakefield,

ex-cheerleader, will soon become Jessica Wake-field, ex-star. And I *will* get around to teaching you that cheer—I promise!"

"What about you, fair Fowler?" asked Winston. "Are you giving up your broomstick and gray dress to return to your drab little life of money, fabulous parties, and designer miniskirts?"

"I most definitely am," said Lila. "I never should have let you all talk me into being a witch in the first place. But you'll never guess who else is giving up her acting career!"

"Who?" asked Annie.

Lila looked around at the expectant faces. She obviously enjoyed being the center of attention. "Paula Perrine!" she announced triumphantly. "But I don't think she knows it yet."

"What are you talking about?" asked Jessica.

"After her performance last night, Mr. Good-man said he was thinking about helping her get an agent in New York. But he got really mad tonight when she didn't show up and didn't even bother to call. I heard him say she wasn't mature enough for a career in the theatre!"

The table was quiet for a few minutes. Annie was beginning to understand what Jessica had meant when she said she felt sorry for Paula. Paula had done a terrible thing to everyone, espe-cially to Jessica. But she would be crushed to find out she wouldn't be going to New York after all.

Jessica turned back to Annie, obviously eager to talk about something besides Paula. "Speaking of New York," she asked, "what kind of model-ing assignment is your mother working on?"

"To tell you the truth, I have trouble keeping them straight. I know it's a series of ads for magazines and television. She's gone to New York twice this month to work on it. She'll finish it up next week."

She sipped her diet soda and thought for a moment. "I really don't know what's so exciting about this particular job," she said finally. "But it must be a good one. I've never seen my mother so thrilled about an assignment. She's practically walking on air!"

*What's in store for Annie and her mother? Find out in Sweet Valley High No. 93, **STEPSISTERS**.*